NASTY

THANK YOU FOR ALL
the support!

— WOMBAT

D1496103

VENGEANCE FLIGHT

T. R. Matson

~ For Nora ~

You are a shining light that can never be extinguished.

Love, Dad

PREFACE

THIS IS A TALE OF REVENGE

Vengeance Flight follows a Navy pilot along his journey of transitioning from flying the E-2C Hawkeye to the F/A-18C Hornet. Along the way, he finds himself caught up in a global, sinister plot of money, power, and greed. Trying to deal with the daily rigors of life on the aircraft carrier and fitting into the new aviation community would be tough enough for anyone. LT Jack "Rattler" Owen faces an unsure future due to a past he cannot seem to get away from. At their core, every human is the same, and even the kindest people among us, when pushed hard enough, have their limits. This is a story of what happens when someone is pushed past that limit and has nothing left to lose. During my decades of military service, I have held the highest levels of security clearances, and because of this, I am required to submit anything I write that I intend for public release, including works of fiction, to the Department of Defense. This manuscript was submitted to the DOD Office of Prepublication and Security Review and was "cleared as amended." My intent in writing *Vengeance Flight* was to allow the reader to follow along in a world that very few will experience firsthand. My intent was to never allow the enemy any advantage, tactical or otherwise, that would put our servicemen and women in harm's way in the future. I have taken great personal pride in ensuring that, above all, this was the case.

I am not Jack Owen, but many others and I have walked in his shoes. I know his feelings and the absolute highs and lows that come with doing the job he was tasked with. While certain squadrons, ships, and other US Navy institutions are mentioned, *Vengeance Flight's* story is fictional, as are the characters mentioned within. Any resemblance to actual people, living or dead, or actual events, is purely coincidental. Thank you for coming on this journey with me, and I hope you enjoy the story of a young man pushed to the breaking point, where he must decide what to do when he has nothing to lose.

— T. R. Matson

PROLOGUE

"Rattler, help!" crackled the number two radio in aircraft 301 as Rattler tried to concentrate on making small corrections flying the ball. This was Field Carrier Landing Practice (FCLPs), and Rattler was trying to make the most of it before heading to the final phase of training in the F/A-18C Hornet.

"Wave off. Wave off," radioed the landing signals officer (LSO) sitting in the small glass shack on the side of the runway.

Rattler immediately pushed his left hand to the max position and momentarily held the pitch of the nose constant as he felt the Hornet climb away from the ground and back to pattern altitude.

"Three-zero-one, Paddles," radioed the LSO.

"Go, Paddles," replied Rattler.

"Hey, buddy. We just got a call from base. Jackie is in trouble. Looks like she has a navigation failure and is lost. Your signal is divert and intercept. Go get her and bring her back to base, buster!" the LSO radioed with urgency.

"Copy all. Three-zero-one departing to the east," Rattler replied as he kept the power in the max detent and cleaned up the gear and flaps.

As Rattler began working with both hands to transition his Hornet from FCLPs to an airborne intercept, he marveled at how far he had come. Less than a year ago, he had taken down the most tyrannical maniac while flying the E-2C Hawkeye, and now he had moved across the country and begun training in the F/A-18C

Hornet aircraft. Less than a week from now, he would finish his carrier landing qualification phase and find out which fleet squadron he was going to join.

Time had flown by, but there was no time to think about that now. Jackie, a nugget student in Rattler's class, was in trouble, and at 0200, there were not a lot of airborne aircraft to help track her down and get her back to base. The weather wasn't too bad, but in the back of his mind, Rattler realized this was the first real test he would face in the Hornet. Everything up until now had just been training under the watchful eye of an instructor. Now it was just him, his machine, and his training.

"Approach control, this is Roman three-zero-one currently climbing to five thousand feet, heading zero-nine-zero for intercept," Rattler radioed.

"Roman three-zero-one, turn right to a heading of one-one-zero. Roman three-one-one is currently twenty miles to the east, altitude indicating between six thousand and ten thousand feet. Our radar is not exactly intercept quality, sir, but we will do our best to get you over there," the approach controller replied.

On the number two radio in aircraft 301, Rattler turned up the volume while getting his air-to-air radar pointed in the right direction. Rattler had to tell himself to calm down, as he could feel his adrenaline starting to climb. There was nothing he was going to be asked to do tonight that he hadn't been trained in.

"Jackie, it's Rattler. Are you up?" Rattler asked.

"Rattler! I'm lost. I've lost my navigation map, and my displays are not working well either. Where are you?" Jackie sounded nervous.

"Don't worry. I've got you on radar, and I will be there soon. What's your fuel state?" Rattler asked.

"Four-point-one," Jackie replied.

"Copy. Stay on your present heading and altitude the best you can, and I will join on you. I'm switching to base frequency real quick but will be back up on the radio soon," Rattler said, trying to calm her down. Flying around in the dark over the ocean with no idea how to get home was not a comfortable feeling, and he could hear the tension in Jackie's voice. He had only known her for a short time since he had started training in the Hornet, but he liked Jackie. She was a hard worker who went to the Naval Academy and came from a long line of naval aviators. It was likely destined almost at birth that she would get her wings of gold and would fly for the Navy.

"Base, three-zero-one, Anyone up?" Rattler asked on the base radio, hoping the squadron duty officer (SDO) was around at this hour.

"Three-zero-one, Gladiator base. Go ahead," the SDO replied.

"Copy. Three-one-one is an emergency aircraft, and I'm enroute to intercept and bring her back to base. The LSOs sent me, and I'm just confirming there are no other assets available right now to assist," Rattler said.

"Uh, well, hang on," the SDO replied, instilling zero confidence in Rattler. He knew that the SDO was a junior student, but he figured there had to be a more senior instructor sitting around the ready room in case of an emergency.

"Three-zero-one from base—yeah, I am the only one here. I just checked in for duty and was told that if anything came up to call the LSO on their cell phone. I'm guessing there is no one else around. Is there anything I can do to help?" replied the SDO.

You've got to be kidding me! Rattler thought. How was it in today's Navy that people cut these kinds of corners and got away with it? There was a solo student out over the ocean and no one around to help, yet someone signed off on this flight schedule. There was no way the LSO would be able to help, because frankly, they were too far away for radio contact, and Rattler wasn't sure Jackie had enough fuel to get from her current position back to the auxiliary field where they had been practicing. How in the hell did he always find himself in these situations?

"Hey, buddy. Here's the deal. I need you to call the LSO and ask him if I should bring three-one-one back to base or over to the auxiliary field, assuming she has the gas for that. When you have an answer, come up on my tactical radio frequency of 127.7, understand?" Rattler said.

"Uh, yes, sir. Copy 127.7 and I will, um, yeah, I will call the LSO now and get back to you," the SDO replied.

"Copy. Three-zero-one out." Rattler switched back to his tactical frequency while he looked at how his radar intercept was working. He would reach Jackie in less than three minutes, and he was looking at his own fuel gauge. *Should be plenty*, he figured, so he kept the power up and kept his scan moving.

"Approach, Roman three-zero-one," Rattler radioed on the number one radio.

"Go ahead, Roman," the controller responded, but it was a different voice, likely the supervisor, Rattler figured, due to the urgent nature of the situation.

"Approach, I know the airspace is empty, but I need to make a direct intercept and join on Roman three-one-one and then fly back to base. I am assuming we will have to set up for a PAR approach to runway two-three left. I need the longest runway, and can you coordinate with the tower and ensure the short field arresting gear is rigged in case we need it?" Rattler asked.

"Roman three-zero-one, copy all, and we will coordinate. Confirm you are radar contact on Roman three-one-one," the controller said.

"Roman three-zero-one radar on Roman three-one-one. Joining now," Rattler replied.

"Roman three-zero-one copy all. We will be standing by," the controller responded.

"Jackie, it's Rattler. I'm on your left side, a little low, joining up. How are you doing?" Rattler asked. He knew keeping everyone calm would ultimately mean the difference between this situation being a success or a complete failure. Jackie likely had vertigo, which was why her altitude and airspeed were not being held constant. Rattler knew Jackie well enough to know that she was a shit-hot pilot who could fly circles around most of the other people in their class. Unfortunately, when vertigo hit, it could take the best pilot and turn them into a mess.

"Rattler, copy that. I have you in sight. I'll be honest. I am really fighting this aircraft right now. It's taken all my energy to just stay straight and level. I've been trying to troubleshoot what's wrong, but I can't get my HUD or MFDs back. I'm on standby instruments and have no map. How far are we off the coast?" Jackie asked.

"Don't worry about that. I've got you now." Rattler moved in closer in position next to 311. "Here's the plan. When you're ready, I want you to give me the lead and try just flying formation off my aircraft. If you are comfortable with that, then I will lead you back to base. We can shoot an instrument approach to get below this cloud deck, and I'll drop you off on the ball and you can fly down to landing. Piece of cake. What's your fuel state?" Rattler asked.

"Okay. Currently, three-point-six, but it's jumping around a little bit on the gauge. I'm good with that plan. You have the lead on the left," Jackie replied.

"Copy. I have the lead on the left." Rattler moved his throttles up a little to help her fall back into position. "The cloud deck is pretty low, so stay in loose formation. I'm going to get us heading back to base, and then if you are not comfortable, we can level off over base before going through the clouds."

"Okay," Jackie replied.

"Approach, three-zero-one holding hands with three-one-one request immediate vector to final for PAR runway two-three-left at NAS Oceana and would like to declare an emergency at this time for aircraft three-one-one," Rattler called.

"Three-zero-one flight, approach control copies. Turn left heading two-seven-zero and descend and maintain four thousand feet. When able, state the nature of the emergency, souls on board, and fuel on board," the approach control replied.

"Three-zero-one flight with three-one-one, which is the emergency aircraft. Three-one-one has electrical malfunctions, and each aircraft has one soul on board and approximately fifteen minutes of fuel remaining," Rattler replied. "I would like to set up for a section approach where I will drop off aircraft three-one-one for a short field arrested landing on two-three-left." He was shooting from the hip here. He hadn't heard back from the SDO, but looking at Jackie's fuel state, he knew that going to the auxiliary field was out of the question, so he was going to have to improvise.

Time was starting to speed up now as Rattler flew the Hornet as smoothly as possible. He had to fly back to base, and hopefully, if he was smooth enough, Jackie would get over the vertigo and be able to stay on his wing through the cloud layer and fly the approach. With her fuel state, there wasn't much more he could do. Just set her up for the best landing possible and hope she could handle it from there. The only other option was ejection, which he tried to push out of his mind.

As they flew the Hornets back toward base, Rattler kept looking over his right shoulder to ensure Jackie was hanging in there. She was doing great, and he was impressed with her ability to handle this situation. He wasn't sure how he would if the roles were reversed.

Approaching fifteen miles from the field, he knew they would have to go through the clouds soon.

"Jackie, how are you feeling?" Rattler asked on tac.

"Much better. I think I can handle this. Fuel low light is on, but I'm assuming we're getting closer. I'm ready to make the approach if it's time," Jackie replied.

"Copy all. It's going to get busy, so just stick with me, and we will use standard comms to get configured for landing. I've already requested a single frequency approach due to the emergency. Tower will come up on our frequency, so you don't have to change the radios at all. Let's do this," Rattler replied.

He went about coordinating with the approach controller like he had done countless times before; but this time, there was much more at stake. Throughout much of the Hornet training, they focused on being a good wingman, so leading this stricken Hornet back to base in the middle of the night and low on gas was not exactly something he was comfortable with. Not that it really mattered much at this point. He was just trying to make quick but smart decisions to get Jackie back on the ground. He could figure out the rest later.

"Roman three-zero-one, report six down and locked," the tower controller said.

"Roman three-zero-one emergency six down and locked. Dash two for short field arrestment, and I will depart the pattern and come in for a landing after she clears," Rattler replied.

"Roman three-zero-one, tower copies. Cleared for one short field arrestment and one low approach, runway two-three-left," the controller replied.

"Jackie, ensure your hook is down," Rattler said on tac.

"It is," she replied.

"What is your fuel state?" Rattler asked.

"Under three-point-zero," Jackie replied.

"Okay, I have the field in sight, and I have the ball in sight. You are on centerline and on glide path. You are cleared for a short field arrestment. When I clear you, I will break away high and to the left. Fly the ball all the way to touchdown, and if you miss the wire, make the decision if you can stop on the runway or not. If not, go around and I will join on you," Rattler exclaimed.

"Okay, sounds good," Jackie replied. "Rattler . . . thank you."

"Thank me at the bar. Three-zero-one detaching," Rattler said as he smoothly broke up and away to the left and slowed down slightly to be able to keep Jackie in sight. He didn't have much fuel of his own, but he would likely try to stay below the clouds and try to land on 23R. As he watched Jackie fly 311 down closer to the runway, his mind was racing, thinking of everything he did and hoping that it was correct. He never heard back from the SDO, but frankly, that did not surprise him at all. He just hoped Jackie would catch the wire and that this night would be over soon.

Aircraft 311 approached the runway and looked okay from Rattler's vantage point high and to the left. Shortly after touchdown, time slowed almost to a stop. It was clear to Rattler that she had not caught the wire. Sparks trailed behind 311 as the arresting hook skidded along the runway. She looked like she was going to try to stop it, and then she swerved hard to the left and back to the right.

"Go around if you need to," Rattler said over tac, which he almost immediately regretted. It was clear that she had blown at least one tire and was having trouble controlling the aircraft. In slow motion, Rattler watched without being able to do anything as aircraft 311 left the paved surface of the runway and was headed straight for the long field arresting gear mechanism. There was no way she could avoid hitting it now and had only one choice.

"EJECT, EJECT, EJECT!" Rattler screamed over the radio.

CHAPTER ONE

Six Months Later

"Shit!" Rattler sat straight up in bed, sweating from the dream.

"Are you okay?" Lying next to him, Sandy reached out to hold his hand.

"Yeah, yeah," Rattler replied, trying to catch his breath.

"Same dream?" Sandy asked.

"Yes," Rattler replied as he realized where he was. "Get some sleep. I'll try to be quiet." He leaned over and kissed Sandy. As he rolled out of bed, his world came back into view. He wasn't in an F-18, and he wasn't even in Virginia anymore. He walked down the hall of his small, rented house in Hanford, California, about twenty-five minutes east of NAS Lemoore, which was the West Coast master jet base. Home to every F/A-18 Hornet and Super Hornet squadron in the Navy.

He got to the kitchen and dug through a cabinet to find a coffee mug from his old squadron. *VAW-117, the Wallbangers* was etched on the side along with the squadron logo and his call sign. *Life has sure come a long way in the past year*, he thought as he poured freshly brewed coffee from his Moccamaster coffee pot. After placing the pot back on the kitchen counter, he made his way to the spare bedroom he used as his office. It was still early, and he needed to get his head straight for the day ahead.

The office was modest, to say the least, but might seem almost barren to some. A small black desk and a single chair sat almost alone, accompanied only by a single bookshelf. The bookshelf held all of Rattler's favorites, from Hemingway to more modern-day thrillers and inspirational tales of military wars fought, won, and lost. Rattler scanned the walls of the room to see a few bits of memorabilia from his career thus far. An etched drawing of a T-45 Goshawk from the day he received his wings hung next to a plaque showing that LT Jack Owen had flown the E-2C Hawkeye for one thousand hours before his first tour of duty was over. Next to that was a bigger picture of all the planes Rattler had flown up to that point in his career, a gift from his parents. And finally, a squadron going-away present, a picture of the E-2C Hawkeye landing on board the ship, which all his squadron mates had signed. He thought back to those times and wondered if he had made the right decision. As he sat down at the desk to check his emails, he looked at a single piece of paper to his left: his official Navy orders directing him to report to VFA-97 at NAS Lemoore upon completion of carrier quals in the F/A-18C Hornet at VFA-106.

Rattler leaned back in his chair, put his feet up on the desk, coffee in hand, and closed his eyes to remember. After the mishap that night trying to get Jackie back safely, there was a brief investigation, in which Rattler was found to not be at fault for the crash of aircraft 311 and, ultimately, the death of his friend. They found that Jackie had blown the left main landing gear tire shortly after missing the arresting cable, and instead of executing a go-around, she opted to keep the aircraft on the runway and try to stop. Improper braking caused the right main landing gear tire to also blow, at which point she should have ejected, but she tried to save the aircraft instead. They determined that she did try to initiate an ejection, but she was too late and impacted the left side arresting gear battery at approximately 110 knots, causing her immediate death.

The news hit the squadron hard, as most were students who had not experienced anything like it before. Rattler had lost friends and dealt with death firsthand just months prior as he tackled his tyrannical commanding officer, knocking him into the turning propeller of a C-2A Greyhound before he could murder "Nails" the Commander of the Air Group (CAG).

Jackie's death was different, though. Rattler's Hawkeye skipper had it coming to him, and frankly, he felt that the final punishment was too swift for the lives and secrets that his skipper sold for his own good. Jackie, on the other hand, was a young, soon-to-be fighter pilot with a very promising career. Her success at the Naval Academy was only a small indication of how bright her future would be. That was cut short, but after her husband, who was a Navy helicopter pilot, was rushed home from deployment for the funeral, life at the squadron got back to normal quickly.

All the students in Rattler's class went back to FCLP training and quickly found themselves one hundred miles off the coast of Virginia, landing both day and night on the aircraft carrier. Everyone passed, and Rattler soon found out that he would be moving to the West Coast to join VFA-97, the Warhawks. He loaded up his Ford F-150 and made the drive west. Stopping along the way, he met up with friends from the past who had been based all around the country. About a week later, he was at his new home and trying to get settled in. All of that seemed like a distant memory at this point, when Rattler was startled out of his daydream by Sandy coming into the office.

"Since I'm up, I'm going to go for a jog," Sandy said.

"Okay. Sorry I woke you," Rattler replied.

"Never be sorry. Anytime I wake up next to you is a good day," she answered with a smile.

"I know it's still early, but maybe put something else on for your jog," Rattler joked.

Sandy winked as she turned around. She was only wearing one of Rattler's squadron T-shirts, and as she walked away, she flipped up the back, essentially flashing Rattler. He had to laugh because, while he loved her completely and she was unbelievably beautiful, her spunky attitude made every minute he spent with her as exciting as the last. Since the time they first met in a hotel in Dubai, Rattler and Sandy had become very close, even given the limited time they could spend together.

During Rattler's training in the Hornet, it seemed like he was constantly on the go. Sandy was still flying as a flight attendant and would try to arrange her schedule to get the most amount of time off and come visit him, but it never felt like it was enough. Goodbyes were never easy, but they did the best they could and were both very invested in making the relationship work.

As Rattler heard Sandy leave the house to go jog, he thought back on everything that had happened since his last deployment. He received orders to transition to fly the F/A-18C Hornet and went to VFA-106 in Virginia Beach, Virginia. There he spent nearly a year getting trained on everything from basic flying to dropping bombs and air-to-air "dog-fighting" before finishing up and getting his carrier qualification, and with it, completion of Hornet training. Upon graduation, he was sent across the country to Lemoore, California, where he would join VFA-97 as they began to work up for their next deployment.

All signs indicated it would be a combat deployment, and Rattler would be thrown into the mix right away after he arrived. While he did very well in Hornet training, he wondered how he would do when he was finally put to the ultimate test. One advantage Rattler had over some of the others was that this was not his first deployment. After serving three combat deployments in the E-2C Hawkeye, Rattler was prepared for time away from home and life at sea. The only thing left to find out was how he would handle being under the stress of real combat in the Hornet. He was told he was joining VFA-97 because they were losing a lot of experience, and while Rattler was still new to the aircraft, the squadron could lean on his leadership experience to help bring the new guys up to speed.

As Rattler sat at his desk, he closed his eyes—once more lost in thought. He had another flight today, which would test his air-to-ground skills. He had been with VFA-97 for a few months now, and he felt like things were starting to click. It was always interesting when a new pilot showed up, and even weirder when that pilot had been in the Navy longer than others, but Rattler was finding his stride and really settling in. He knew that Sandy was going to have to leave soon, and there would only be one more opportunity for them to spend time together before he left on deployment, and that wouldn't be for another month. She was still working as a flight attendant and lived in Australia, so they had very few chances to see each other, which was something Rattler was concerned about ever since they had met. He tried to enjoy their time together and appreciate every second, but he also had to focus on getting better in the aircraft. Lucky for him, Sandy understood and very much supported this. Often, he would return from a long day at the squadron to find her lounging by the pool, working on her tan, but then she would make dinner and try to make the time they had together special. He really appreciated that about her, and it set her even further apart from his ex-wife.

He couldn't dwell on that too much right now because he had to get his head right for his flight. Today was a two-ship, low-level ingress flight to a pop attack—a very dynamic flight that would likely only last about an hour and a half but would feel like it was much quicker. Rattler hadn't slept much the night prior thinking about this flight, not because of the tactics or anything like that, which he was confident in, but because of his flight lead.

LCDR Troy "Toad" Kirby was the flight lead for today's flight. Most likely, Toad got his call sign because of the huge wart on his face that resembled that of a frog. Of course, as someone new to the squadron, Rattler knew better than to ask because he didn't want to draw any more attention to himself than absolutely required. In fact, he felt like he had already drawn too much attention from Toad from day one.

CHAPTER TWO

Rattler sat nervously in the driver's seat of his truck in front of VFA-97, home of the Warhawks. Two days prior, he had finished his drive across the country from Virginia to California; and yesterday, he had checked into his new home. He had three-year orders to the Warhawks and was ready to get started. He was on his own, with Sandy being on a long trip, his parents' home in New Jersey, and all his friends in different squadrons. He had become so used to relying on his friends that it was weird to be sitting here essentially without a support network. Naval aviation is very much about looking out for one another, and while Rattler knew or hoped he would eventually build that network here at the Warhawks, right now he felt alone.

Instinctively, he reached into his flight suit pocket and felt for his dog tags. Attached to them was the small cross given to him by his aunt. It was right where he expected it to be and immediately brought him peace. He knew that while this was not going to be easy, he had been through much worse, and he would be successful. It was time to finally live his childhood dream. He had wanted to fly fighters since the day he watched the Blue Angels with his father, and now he was a qualified Hornet pilot, ready to start the next phase in life.

Yesterday, he had checked in, met with most of the officers, and got the lay of the land. Today was going to be his first flight. Having trained on the East Coast, flying out west was relatively new to him, and his commanding officer understood that. CDR Michael "Professor" Burns was in charge of VFA-97 for the next six months.

He was scheduled to leave the squadron right before they left on deployment, which he was not happy about. He was a strong man in both stature and leadership and wanted to take the men and women he trained with to combat.

The Navy had another idea. They had given Professor orders to a shore tour, even though he requested to extend. "Needs of the Navy" is what they call it, and there was nothing he could do about it. Professor took great pride in the fact that he was going to make sure the men and women of VFA-97 were as prepared as they could be to go to war. After meeting with him, Rattler found out that Professor would lead him on his first flight to get comfortable with the area.

"Listen, I am going to treat you like a new guy, but only when it comes to the jet," Professor said. "I know your leadership, and I am very aware of your history. I need help to ensure the enlisted men and women of this command are ready for what is waiting for them on the aircraft carrier. When it comes to the jet, I know you can produce a lot, but I need you to follow the progression that is in place. Tomorrow, we will fly together, and all I need you to do is check the weather and notice to airmen (NOTAMs). I will take care of the rest."

"Yes, sir." Rattler stood to leave his commanding officer's office.

"Son, your work ethic and reputation precede you. Keep your head down and your nose clean and you will do great here," Professor finished.

"Yes, sir," Rattler replied on his way out of the office.

Rattler couldn't help but think about what the skipper meant while he sat in his truck in a mostly empty parking lot. It was early in the morning, and most members of the squadron wouldn't be in for a while. Rattler wanted to get a jump start on the day and be prepared for the brief. *Early is never a bad thing*, Rattler thought as he got out

7

of the truck and made his way to the ready room. He knew that was a good place to start since it was the meeting place for the aircrew and where most hung out when they weren't flying or doing their ground jobs. As he made his way up the stairwell to the second floor of the giant hangar that housed VFA-97 jets, Rattler saw the history of the squadron. From their roots, it was clear to him that this squadron had been places and had participated in many conflicts around the globe. He vowed to make the men and women of the Warhawks—past, present, and future—proud. Hopefully, he could put his past behind him and start moving forward.

Looking for a computer, Rattler walked past the empty ready room and found the operations office. As he logged on to check the weather and NOTAMs, he noticed someone come in behind him. Rattler stood as he turned around.

"Sir, I'm LT Owen, Rattler," Rattler said, extending his hand to the officer he did not recognize from the previous day.

"I see. I am LCDR Kirby, call sign Toad," the man said. "How about you come into my office so we can get the formal introductions out of the way?"

"Yes, sir," Rattler replied, although he felt it was odd they couldn't talk where they were. There was no one else around, and so far, everyone in the squadron seemed great and pretty relaxed. Rattler shrugged it off as he walked to the much smaller office marked "Safety Officer," where he assumed Toad would ask him to sit. He did not. In fact, the tone for the meeting was set immediately.

"No need to sit since I will get straight to the point," Toad began. "I have been in the Navy for fifteen years and four at the Naval Academy before that. That is almost two decades of honor, courage, and commitment running through my veins. The Navy is my life, and her traditions and code of conduct are the foundation that I live by every day. I will be frank with you; what did you say your call sign was?"

"Rattler, sir."

"Ah, yes. I will be frank with you, Rattler. I have never been very impressed with pilots who transition from other communities and try to come over and fly fighters. I figure if you are good enough to be a fighter pilot, then they should have given you fighters out of flight school. To get them later in your career is simply a gift and doesn't sit well with me. You will be flying some of the best in the Warhawks, and I just don't see you being successful here. You will most likely be behind the aircraft, and I will not allow you to drag us down. I have already conveyed my concerns to the skipper that we shouldn't have wasted a spot on you prior to this combat deployment. This isn't going to be like the deployments you've been on in the past. This time, it is real, and you cannot hesitate, or people will die."

Rattler stood a little taller now and soaked in every word from Toad. He couldn't tell if this was some sort of horrible motivational speech or if Toad really felt the way he did. Either way, it wouldn't matter. People had second-guessed Rattler in the past, and he just kept working hard to prove them wrong. *This will be no different*, he thought.

"Also, one last thing," Toad said. "Your E-2C skipper was my squad leader at the Naval Academy. He was an amazing man, a man who was forged on the same foundation that I was. Obviously, the Navy has not released all the details, but I will have you know that I took his loss very personally. The Navy lost a great man in him. I know this is just your second day here, and maybe you will prove me wrong, but I doubt it. I believe in being upfront and honest, so there you have it. I believe you have a flight to prepare for, and I will not keep you anymore. Dismissed."

"Sir, thank you, and I can tell this is going to be the start of a wonderful friendship," Rattler replied sarcastically as he left the office.

CHAPTER THREE

Rattler finished getting ready for work and was ready to leave when Sandy returned from her jog. After a little playful banter, he walked out to the garage and paused momentarily, looking over the car parked there—a 1967 Shelby GT500, given to him by his dad after he returned from his last deployment. It was Rattler's first car that he sold when he went off to college, but his father was able to find it and buy it back. The car was a mess and needed a lot of work, but it ran well. He could almost still see the faded blue paint under all the dust and grime. Looking at the car reminded him of summers working in his parents' mechanic shop. He learned a lot about cars and even more about life during that time, but mostly, it was his parents' hard work ethic that sat with him this morning.

While he had not gotten much sleep, he did know that he had prepared for this flight and was confident he would do well. He knew Toad was going to be hard on him in the brief and would keep all extra communication between the two planes to a minimum, but Rattler knew how to be professional; and while it would have been a lot more fun to fly the mission with someone else, he would get through it. He ran his hand over the car before hopping into his truck and setting off for base.

Lemoore was a departure from anywhere else he had been stationed so far, with miles and miles of dairy farms and all the sights and smells that came with it. While it provided little in the way of nightlife, Lemoore was a great place to fly. Just west of the Sierra mountains, there were many live bombing ranges and an abundance of airspace for the Navy fighter squadrons to hone their skills. Before he knew it, Rattler was at the squadron and parking next to another pilot who just arrived.

LT Mike "Maestro" Smith was getting out of the family minivan as Rattler pulled up. Maestro was the opposite of Rattler in almost every way. He was married and had three children already, with another on the way. Maestro got his call sign because he studied music in college as opposed to the more traditional engineering route that a lot of pilots chose. While on paper they were different, they hit it off immediately and had been close since the day Rattler walked in the door.

"Hey, buddy. How are you doing?" Maestro asked as he got out of the van.

"Doing great, man. Got the family van today, huh?" Rattler replied.

"Yeah, the wife took the other car to the gym. She said she would swap them later. Nothing like driving a minivan to make me feel like a real fighter pilot, huh?" Maestro joked. "You ready for this flight today?"

"As ready as I'll ever be," Rattler replied as the two walked into the squadron. Rattler knew this was going to be a long day, but he kept his mind on the task at hand.

"Dude, don't let that idiot get to you," Maestro said. "He does this to everyone. Sure, he's a little butt hurt about your E-2C skipper, but death is part of this job, and accidents happen. He should know that as well as anyone else. In the meantime, just deal with Toad. We all do, and no one likes flying with him."

"Will do, buddy," Rattler replied. Maestro was the person he felt the closest to in the squadron. Trust had to be earned, but Rattler could see that their friendship would likely pass the test of time.

Rattler and Maestro parted ways as they got to the second floor of the hangar. Maestro was the squadron duty officer (SDO) for the day, and Rattler was off to the mission planning room. Rattler laughed to himself as he walked into the secure room they used for mission planning. While there was nothing particularly classified about today's mission, this room was where all the computers were placed. Rattler set about building the kneeboard card both pilots would use for the flight that would have all the important call signs, frequencies, and contingency plans for the mission. It also had a fuel planning section, so both pilots could quickly and easily see how they were doing on fuel. There was no airborne fuel today, so in-flight refueling would not be a factor, and Toad and Rattler would have to keep a watchful eye on what fuel they carried with them. They needed to set predetermined fuel numbers that, when reached, would signal them to knock off the flight and head back to base.

The weather in Lemoore was usually consistent, but there was always a chance that fog would roll in this time of year, and if that happened, they would have to divert to another base. Crews in the past had gotten very low on gas during these situations, and Rattler did not want to highlight himself by making that mistake. Ultimately, Toad would be the flight lead today, but Rattler was trying his best to be a good wingman, which wasn't easy when he didn't like his flight lead at all.

The brief and preflight went surprisingly smoothly, as it seemed like Toad was in a rare, good mood. Rattler was feeling confident as he fired up the engines of aircraft 310 and taxied to the Marshall area. He got there first, which was a small victory for a wingman. It's always good when you are early, and your flight lead doesn't need to wait on you. As Toad taxied up, the aircraft checked in on their tactical frequency and began their taxi to the runway.

Today would be a standard interval takeoff, and as Toad ran up the engines on his aircraft and released the brakes, Rattler counted to four and did the same. Immediately selecting full afterburner, Rattler felt the jolt of power come out of his relatively light Hornet. Today, they each had four MK76 practice bombs, which at only twenty-five pounds each, weighed significantly less than what the Hornet could handle. Rattler quickly got a radar lock on Toad and within a short time was joined up in formation as their flight headed east to the bombing range.

Rattler had a moment of calm during the transit to the range to reflect on how his Hornet transition was coming along. He thoroughly enjoyed flying the plane, but who wouldn't? It was like owning the fastest, sleekest race car that you didn't have to pay for. He was feeling particularly blessed to have gotten the transition from the E-2C Hawkeye, but, unfortunately, not all his friends felt the same way. Some people from Rattler's past seemed to have alienated him, perhaps thinking he was a traitor of sorts for leaving the Hawkeye community, but Rattler saw the opportunity and didn't want to live his life with regrets. Looking back on his experience, the training was challenging, but he was glad he did it. He was at the point now that he was starting to feel like the Hornet was an extension of his own body, and he noted how much more quickly that happened in the Hornet than in the Hawkeye. It could be the design of the plane or the hours of flying and deployments' worth of experience that Rattler already had, but at any rate, he was happy with how it was going.

In the cockpit, his hands were manipulating switches subconsciously, and he was relatively ahead of the jet as he switched sides to be on the right side of Toad's aircraft for the ingress to the target. Both aircraft had switched up to the range controller, call sign "Ripper," who would ultimately allow them to drop their practice ordnance today. Ripper was the overall safety officer for the mission, and if he said to abort, then Toad and Rattler would immediately discontinue their attack, safe up their master arm switches, and climb to a safe altitude.

"Ripper, Hawk Flight up on range control," Toad said from the lead jet as the formation approached the initial point for ingress to the target.

"Hawk Flight, Ripper is up. Go ahead with check-in," Ripper replied from the small shack where he could see the target and watch the aircraft roll in before dropping their ordnance.

"Hawk flight is two by F/A-18C aircraft, each with four by MK76 and twenty minutes of playtime," Toad replied.

"Hawk flight, Ripper copies all. Ripper will have over range safety, and all cleared hot and abort calls will be made in the clear," replied Ripper. "Report IP inboard."

"Hawk flight copies," Toad replied.

Both aircraft now went into tactical mode as Toad and Rattler went quietly about their individual jobs. Toad's job was to lead the flight through the proper waypoints to hit their time on target. While this was all simulated and training for their mission, they did their best to act as they would if conducting a similar strike in Afghanistan on their deployment.

Rattler's role for this mission was both as an attack aircraft and a support role. He knew Toad would be more task saturated with ensuring the flight was in the right place at the right time, so it was critical that Rattler kept in perfect formation and kept a lookout for surface-to-air missile launches or enemy aircraft. Rattler could be the final person to catch either, which could mean the difference between life and death. Today, Rattler knew there would be no such missiles or enemy aircraft, but he did his best to keep his eyes moving and stay ahead of the aircraft.

Approaching the designated point, the formation split slightly, giving Toad some spacing so his aircraft would reach the target first. The goal here was for his bombs to impact and explode before Rattler's jet arrived on target. There were two reasons for this. First, it would allow Rattler to adjust his bomb drop based on where Toad's hit; and second, and even more importantly, Rattler's jet would not be in the fragmentation area when the bomb exploded, which would minimize the chances of it getting damaged.

"Hawk one-one, popping," Toad said over the range frequency.

"Hawk, continue," Ripper replied.

"Hawk one-one in," Toad replied as he rolled his jet into a 125-degree overbank to set up for the attack run.

"Hawk cleared hot," Ripper replied, ultimately giving Toad permission to release his MK76 bombs. Toad reached up with his left hand and moved the master arm switch to the arm position, and then he made his final adjustments to his heading before pushing down the "pickle" button on the stick and immediately pulling aft on the stick and selecting full power.

"Hawk one-one, off safe two away," Toad said.

Immediately following this, Rattler repeated the sequence of being cleared hot and arming up his weapons. He also released two MK76 bombs and executed the escape maneuver. Toad then entered the "wagon wheel" pattern over the target to roll in one more time and drop the remaining two MK76 bombs before heading home. Rattler followed, and as he rolled in for his second and final bombing run, he noted the position of Toad's jet just ahead, climbing. The moment Rattler pushed down on the pickle switch, releasing his bombs, the radio came to life as Rattler looked up and saw a fireball come out of Toad's jet.

"Hawk one-one declaring an emergency. I have a compressor stall on the left motor, and I am shutting it down," Toad called.

"Ripper copies all, and the range is cold. Ensure your weapons are safe and you are cleared to exit the airspace to the west. Good luck, gentlemen," Ripper replied.

Rattler broke the silence. "Hawk one-one from one-two on tac."

"Go," Toad replied, clearly busy.

"I'm a little low and on your left side. I'll join in loose cruise and standby for whatever you need. I'm breaking out the checklist now," Rattler called.

"Copy. The motor is shut down. I need you to ensure that the fire is out," Toad replied. In the world of ejection seat aircraft, things like this were handled a little differently than when Rattler was flying the Hawkeye.

As he got closer, Rattler could tell that Toad had already gone through the memory items because his hook was down. This was a critical step since he would attempt a field arrestment and egress immediately on landing. Toad was busy coordinating with the air traffic controllers to immediately get back to Lemoore and set up for a landing. Rattler had little to do and knew better than to interject too much. He moved his aircraft closer in to check out his flight lead and noticed something peculiar. While Toad had shut down the motor and likely blew the fire bottle to extinguish the fire, his jet was still burning.

"Hawk one-one from one-two," Rattler called.

"Go, but I'm a little busy here. In fact, why don't you just detach and head to base on your own," Toad said—although Rattler ignored it, as it would violate the squadron operating procedures (SOPs) and, frankly, didn't make any sense.

"Toad, I am behind and below you, out of the way. Don't worry about me, but you are still on fire. Confirm you blew the fire bottle," Rattler said, trying to back up his lead.

"Rattler JUDY!" Toad screamed, indicating in fighter pilot lingo that he wanted Rattler to shut up.

Rattler retarded his throttles slightly to move further aft of the lead jet and made sure he had a radar lock so he wouldn't lose him.

He sat in his cockpit all alone and dropped his mask to take a breath of fresh air. Shaking his head, he thought to himself how much of an ass Toad was being. It was clear from day one that Toad didn't like him, but this was getting out of hand. His fucking jet was on fire, and if nothing else, Rattler knew that a good wingman should always be in position and tell the lead when they were on fire.

At this point, he was starting to not care what happened to Toad and the jet. They were flying as fast as possible back to Lemoore, where Toad would set up for a field arrestment. Rattler put his Hornet on autopilot, keeping Toad in sight but also giving him some space. He pulled out his pocket checklist for the emergency on-scene commander and began reviewing it. He knew that if Toad had to eject, Rattler would take over the Search and Rescue (SAR) role immediately until he was relieved by a better asset. Looking at his fuel, he figured at a conservative rate he could loiter for about twenty minutes before he would have to land.

Ahead and above, Toad was busy thinking through his procedures. He had done everything, but nothing worked. The red FIRE light was still illuminated, and he knew he would have to get out of the aircraft quickly on the runway. He had to balance flying as fast as he could to get to the field but then also slowing down in time to ensure his aircraft was in the perfect landing attitude to catch the wire. He put everything he didn't need into his helmet bag and was finally close enough to pull the other throttle to idle and configure for landing.

"Tower, Hawk one-one three down and locked for field arrestment," Toad said over the radio.

"Hawk one-one, you are cleared to land runway three-two-right. Crash, fire, and rescue are standing by," Tower replied.

"Hawk one-one cleared to land," Toad said.

Rattler still stayed behind Toad's aircraft slightly and configured to match his speed to keep an eye on him. He had remained quiet on the radio ever since the Judy call, and now he played through his mind what would likely happen. He had plenty of fuel and would just depart the pattern and reenter for the overhead break to land on the parallel runway after Toad stopped. He watched the best he could as Toad's jet hit the runway just prior to the arresting wire.

A quick flashback of Jackie's jet exploding back at VFA-106 hit Rattler, and he began to sweat. He pushed the thought out of his mind as he saw Toad's jet come to a stop and the canopy immediately open as the fire trucks started hosing down the aircraft. He saw Toad jump out and run away, and although he was doing what he should, Rattler couldn't help but think that Toad looked like a coward the way he ran, even from eight hundred feet in the air. Happy that everything worked out, Rattler briefly laughed and called tower.

"Tower, Hawk one-two request departure to the west for the carrier break for three-two-left," Rattler called.

"Hawk one-two cleared as requested. Report the initial," Tower replied as Rattler engaged full afterburner and selected gear and flaps up. *Might as well have a little fun today,* he thought as he saw the airspeed rapidly climbing.

CHAPTER FOUR

"Rattler, can I talk to you?" Toad asked, sticking his head in the ready room where Rattler and Maestro were talking.

"Yes, sir," Rattler replied, catching Maestro's eye as he walked away. Rattler followed Toad down to his office. He knew that he had likely overstepped his boundaries during the flight and would probably catch hell for it. He wasn't too worried. He had been in the Navy for over six years now; this wouldn't be the first time he was yelled at or even grounded if that's what it came to. Rattler knew how to take his licks and roll with them. The flight hadn't exactly been a success, but they did execute the ingress flawlessly, and Rattler received word that his practice bombs all got very close to bull's-eye hits, which he was happy about.

"Sit down," Toad said. Rattler moved to the chair next to Toad's desk and sat nervously. For some reason, Toad had that effect on him, and he didn't like it. It was something he was going to have to figure out if they were going to work together in the squadron, especially on deployment.

"Quite a flight today, huh?" Toad started. "I want to clear the air. I spoke with the skipper, and I am not proud of my behavior in the air. You were just trying to help, and I should not have acted that way. I think this goes further back to when you checked into the squadron. I was still pretty upset about losing a mentor, and I took that out on you. A good leader does not do that. I still don't know the details, as they have all been classified at the highest levels, but it was wrong of me to assume any of it was your fault. At the Naval Academy, they teach us about leadership and the correct way to lead your subordinates, and what I did was not correct. I acted out of emotion instead of using rational thought. Today, in the jet, I did the same. We are going on deployment together soon, and we need to operate together and trust each other. I just wanted to tell you that I'm sorry for what I did." Toad reached out his hand to shake Rattler's hand.

Rattler stood and shook Toad's hand. He could tell the conversation was over, so he turned to walk away. He hadn't reached the door yet when Toad said, "Rattler, thanks again for your help up there today. Hope to see you and your girl at the squadron party this Friday."

"Yes, sir," Rattler replied.

As Rattler walked down the hallway past all the squadron spaces, he was still in a daze. Everyone seemed busy taking care of something, and most didn't notice him at all. He decided it was time to go get a workout in at the gym, so he grabbed his bag and headed to the truck. His mind was racing again. There was nothing to indicate he shouldn't take what Toad said in the office at anything other than face value, but he still felt uneasy. He just wanted his past to be his past, and he wanted to move forward, but that clearly wasn't going to happen so easily. One thing was for sure: an hour at the gym throwing around heavy weights would help. Ever since his young football days, he always felt great after a hard workout, and he knew that was just what the doctor ordered today. He hopped into his truck, started it, and turned the radio up. Heavy-metal music filled his ears, and he already felt better.

CHAPTER FIVE

The week went by quickly, and before Rattler knew it, he was heading home early Friday afternoon. All the officers were getting together at the skipper's house, and Rattler had to get home, shower, and grab Sandy before heading back to base. Rattler drove rather quickly from the base to his house on the country roads of Lemoore, which he seemed to have all to himself. The area was mainly dairy farms, and it amazed him how quickly the sound of jets faded away when he drove off base. As his ears filled with music from the truck and his nose filled with the ever-present aroma of cow fields, it almost seemed like he lived in two different worlds. Before he knew it, he was pulling into the driveway and heading inside. He found Sandy getting ready in the bathroom, and he hopped in the shower after only a quick kiss. He didn't want to be late, and Sandy could tell. It didn't take her long to transform from sweaty workout clothes to drop-dead gorgeous and ready to mingle. Maybe it was a byproduct of her country upbringing or maybe her job as a flight attendant, but either way, Rattler knew he would not be waiting on her.

After a quick shower and change of clothes, Rattler and Sandy were back in his truck, heading to base. "Are you looking forward to this?" Sandy asked.

"Honestly, not really. Something feels different here. When I was in the Wallbangers, I loved hanging out in my spare time, but now it just feels different," Rattler replied.

"Well, you have been working a lot," Sandy said.

"Yeah, sorry about that. I know that you are only in town for a limited time, and I really need to maximize my time with you. It's just, with all the studying, planning, and flying, not to mention my ground jobs, it seems like there aren't enough hours in the day."

"Never apologize for your hard work," Sandy said. "Your hard work is what got you here, and I am so proud of you. This is just a short part of our lives together, and we will get through it. We will make the most of what we can, and I will visit you as much as possible once you are on deployment. I would never want to get in the way of your dreams, because that would just lead to you resenting me. I am very happy to spend the time I have with you, so let's just have a good time tonight and make the best of it."

"You're right." Rattler's gaze drifted across the dairy fields. He couldn't shake the feeling that something just wasn't the same here. He had heard people say that your first fleet squadron was always special, and you would never feel the same way again, no matter how long you stayed in. He was hoping to build the same strong bonds at the Warhawks as he had with the Wallbangers, but it was off to a slow start. Maybe it was the operational tempo of the squadron getting ready for a deployment or maybe just different people. For all he knew, he got lucky in the Wallbangers, and maybe it would never be the same.

His daydreaming stopped as he approached the main gate of the base and presented his military ID to the gate guard. The gate guard, in turn, returned a sharp salute. As Rattler accelerated through the barricades, he noted the guard had noticed Sandy in the passenger seat. *What's not to notice?* he thought as he admired her sitting there with a golden-brown tan, wearing a sundress and sandals; she looked more like a model than anything else. Rattler was a lucky man.

He navigated his truck through the base to the housing area, which included rows and rows of standard-looking houses that were clearly all built from the same floor plan. In typical military fashion, the houses were built as quickly as possible and left little room for them to be unique. The size of an individual's house tended to grow along with their rank, and as he approached the area where his skipper's house sat, he could tell he was clearly in the senior officer area.

Even with each house basically being the same, it seemed like each officer, or maybe their spouse, set out to make theirs stand out. Squadron decorations showed who was who, and many houses were clearly decorated for returning servicemen and women. Rattler thought about how happy those families must be. Returning from a deployment was almost always a great feeling. Long times away from family usually led to very happy times catching up when you got home.

This naturally brought Rattler's thoughts back to the last time he returned from deployment. While he had fond memories of enjoying San Diego with Sandy, he had to also remember that he returned home to no more wife and to the memories of watching his skipper meet his demise after trying to take down their Hawkeye squadron. Those visions would likely not leave his mind for a while, if ever.

Rattler put the truck in park and walked around to open the door for Sandy. He could tell that while he was not late, the party had already begun. From the backyard, the sounds of music and storytelling were in full swing. Through the front window, he could see a group of women huddled around the kitchen talking, likely trying to get away from the constant stories of flying that were going on in the backyard. This would be Sandy's first time at a Warhawk squadron party, and he was a bit nervous. He knew she would be able to handle herself, but he was concerned she would see a life she wasn't interested in.

"Ready for this?" he asked as he opened the door.

"Of course, honey. I know how to put on a pretty face and play the game. It's what I do for a living. You don't think I like to be polite to all those ungrateful passengers all the time, do you?" she asked. "Remember, at the end of the night, we are going home together for a nightcap and time together on the couch. This is all part of the game that must be played if you want to be taken seriously in this world. I know this isn't you, but do your best. I believe you are destined for great things, but sometimes we just have to grit our teeth and get through the things we'd rather skip."

"You really are something special," Rattler said as he kissed her and led her to the front door.

The night went exactly how Rattler expected. Stories of flying and very little else. The wives tended to keep their distance and talk about whatever it was that wives talked about while drinking wine. The skipper's house was perfect, and it gave the impression that he had the perfect life. Some would think that was true. He was the commanding officer of a fighter squadron in the Navy, which on the surface seemed to be the goal of every other pilot in the squadron, but Rattler knew better. He had become very good at reading people, and he could tell there was tension between the skipper and his wife. Maybe it was stress from a lifetime of being apart, or maybe it was that he felt cheated by not being able to go on this upcoming deployment, but at any rate, the tension was there. Rattler kept his mouth shut, for the most part, and listened to the stories. Most were the same stories he had heard before, just with different names; the Navy tended to be that way.

Then something caught his attention.

Rattler had made his way to the backyard to grab another beer and found himself around the small firepit. Seven of the Warhawk pilots were standing around listening to the executive officer (XO) tell a story from his previous tour as a department head. CDR Scott "Dice" Bailey had been the XO of the Warhawks for some time now and was rapidly approaching his change of command prior to deployment. Dice was a larger-than-life individual who got his call sign by always taking risks. Some of those risks were in the air, but in a Navy that would normally frown on that behavior, Dice seemed to thrive. He came from a naval aviation background, and his father was a well-known fighter pilot of the Vietnam era. Dice had progressed through the ranks on a normal timeline and had flown the F/A-18C for all of it.

"So, we are in the middle of blue water operations with no divert options available," Dice was saying. "We were a four-ship division of Hornets that was setting up for an air-to-air training mission against four Super Hornets. We figured this would be an easy fight since two of the Super Hornets were 'five wet' tankers and really couldn't maneuver very easily. We set up in a wall formation and went about our tasking. Each fighter had their own role. As I was working my radar out ahead and making sure all my checklists were complete, the lead called for a formation shift. Basically, just a ten-degree heading change that I put in. I glanced quickly out to my right to ensure I was where I was supposed to be and then went back to work.

"What I didn't notice was that number three in the formation hadn't changed heading, and now we were on a collision course. It was nighttime, and we were all on goggles. Something caught my eye at the last second, and time stopped," the XO continued, with each pilot hanging on his every word. "Number three was not at the correct altitude. If he was, I could have passed over him safely. Instead, I executed a full aft stick pull, and we still impacted. My fuel tank went right through the tails of his Hornet, and my plane immediately had flight control problems. I thought I was going to have to eject immediately, but I took a deep breath and analyzed what I was dealing with. The coordination that was involved in getting both aircraft safely on the ground that night was nothing short of a miracle."

The XO went on to describe from his perspective the same night that Rattler, who was flying in the Hawkeye in the Wallbangers at the time, had launched on an alert and ended up having to stay airborne so long that his left motor shut down from fuel starvation shortly after landing.

All Rattler could do was listen. He was playing that night back through his mind, and it was interesting to hear the different perspectives. The only people in the backyard who were airborne that night were himself and his XO. Their stories were very different, but the result was the same. In the end, it was the hard work of everyone involved that allowed all involved to be safe and fly again.

After the XO had finished, he looked over at Rattler. "The E-2C Hawkeye that night really saved our asses."

"Yes, sir. Aircraft six-zero-one," Rattler replied, to which the XO's eyes got big. His brain was processing slower due to the beers, but he was standing in front of the pilot who had provided a means to coordinate his safe landing years prior. Once he finished calculating everything, the XO asked. "Was that you?"

"Yes, sir," Rattler replied.

"I heard you flew that plane to basically empty fuel tanks," The XO said.

Rattler smiled. "Not quite empty, sir."

"Gentlemen," the XO said, facing the rest of the pilots who had gathered around. "I would not be standing here today if it weren't for Rattler. I know he is new to our squadron and comes from a less-than-typical past, but you can learn from the things he has done and seen. That night he pushed the envelope to the absolute maximum, and if he hadn't, I would not have made it home. There was no way I could have coordinated all that airborne fuel to get me on the ground. What he did was an extremely brave thing—launching in a plane without the ability to refuel airborne, knowing he was going to have to stay up as long as possible. Make no mistake about it. In my mind, that act alone was nothing short of heroic."

He hugged Rattler. "Son, if you ever even think of buying a beer in my presence again, I will kick your ass!"

The rest of the night was a blur of good times and squadron comradery that Rattler enjoyed. When they finally made it home, Rattler was happy to be in bed next to the woman he loved, but he couldn't help but feel a little better about his future in the Warhawks. Maybe he would prove others wrong, and his second squadron could be as good as his first.

CHAPTER SIX

The old man sat in his private office behind a large wooden desk. The room was filled with memorabilia from a career in the Navy that spanned three decades. It began at the Naval Academy, where the bonds formed during those four years lasted a lifetime. Some had moved on to other things, while others had passed away, but the core was still together.

The man logged into his computer and bypassed various passwords and firewalls to reach the sensitive information—the report, the real report of what had happened to his protégé, CDR Michael Maddox, a freshman at the academy when they first met. The old man saw great potential in him, and he was on track, but that was all over now due to his untimely death.

As the old man pored over the report in front of him, he read about the information that had been planted, which in turn large sums of money were funneled into an offshore account. The purpose was twofold. First, it would show the vulnerabilities of the Navy, which would cause the government to increase military spending. While the organization's members would profit from the information sold, they would also profit from the highly lucrative contracts that would be awarded to them, due to insider information, to help fix the problem. The members of the group would each have a bank account in a false name waiting for them. When the time was right, they could disappear and live very comfortably for the rest of their years.

One of the biggest hurdles to get over was the lives that the information would put at risk. This was easy for the old man because he had been around for a while and had been taught by the best. His indoctrination, if you could call it that, started long before his time at the Naval Academy, when he would listen to the meetings his father would have with his "friends." When he was young, he wrote it off as old men talking, but as he reached his high school years, he could tell that his father was a very powerful man—a man you did not mess with, and one who others respected. At that point, he wanted to emulate his father and gain that same power over others.

As the man adjusted himself at his desk and finished the report, his rage grew. The plan was working perfectly, as they had planted agents in all areas of the Navy to research, highlight, and even create problems the Navy would be forced to fix once they were exploited. The Hawkeye community was essential to control, as it had the ability to affect so many other aspects of the Navy—in the air, sea, and subsea areas. CDR Maddox was well on his way to setting the wheels in motion to get the funding that would set himself and his peers up for a very long time. The money that would come in from the Hawkeye upgrade program was enough for them to disappear and sip fruity drinks on a beach somewhere for the rest of their lives.

That was all before some hotshot pilot got in the way. The old man took a deep breath and switched his gaze to another computer screen that had one picture on it. It was the official officer photo from the naval record of LT Jack Owen. The old man glared at the screen as he tried to figure out if this lieutenant knew what he was doing or just stepped into the wrong pile of shit. The amount of money and time he had cost the organization would be impossible to recover. At this point, they had to abandon their work in that area and focus on the other aspects of their plan that were still on track. That being said, the old man was not one to let things go. He still remembered every person who wronged him in the past and kept a list of those for whom he felt revenge was appropriate. LT Owen was now on that list.

The old man stood and walked over to his bar. Various dark liquids presented themselves in very expensive ways, but he reached past them all to the back. He knew exactly what he wanted, and after placing two ice cubes in a glass, he half filled it with his favorite. After swirling the liquid, which was a habit of his, he went back to his desk and finished reading the report. It was then that he read the part about CDR Maddox's final demise. The old man closed his eyes and leaned back in his chair.

He thought back on meeting CDR Maddox's family and their times together. Maddox had a beautiful wife and children who would be alone now. While they would be compensated by the military, it would be a drop in the bucket compared to the retirement that the commander had set up for them. Angered more by this, the old man finished his drink, set the glass down on the desk, and picked up his phone. He typed in the phone number by heart, which was not a contact in his phone, and simply typed "Operation Snake Bite is a go." Revenge would come quickly.

CHAPTER SEVEN

"Three-zero-five Hornet Ball four-point-six, Owen," Rattler radioed as he guided his F/A-18 Hornet to a good start and quickly transitioned from an inside instrument scan to an outside scan of the Fresnel lens. Rattler loved this part of flying. The precision and the concentration it took to put a modern fighter aircraft into the small piece of sky needed to land it on the ship successfully was critical. Another piece that was critical and separated Navy pilots from all others was that the ship was always moving. The ramp behind the ship didn't care how your day was going or how much sleep you got. It didn't care if you had a bad flight or if there was stress at home. It would kill you in an instant if you let it, and that was that. It didn't matter if it was your first landing or your one thousandth landing, and that was what made flying around the boat the great equalizer.

The LSO in Rattler also understood the relationship between ball flying and his reputation around the ship, so naturally, he took it seriously. Sure, the late-night flying around the darkness of Lemoore wasn't the most exciting thing to do, but Sandy was back on the road flying her trips, so he was in no hurry to get back to an empty house.

The minor corrections came quickly to Rattler, and before he knew it, his Hornet slammed down on the runway. He immediately added full power and rotated his jet airborne again. Scanning ahead of him, he found his interval and leveled off at pattern altitude. The Hornet was very different from the Hawkeye, especially when it came to landing the aircraft. The wingspan was much smaller, and the power was pretty much on demand, not that the Hawkeye was underpowered. The biggest difference was the lack of P-factor from the turning propellers. Every time you added power in the Hawkeye, the nose wanted to come up, and right when you took power off, the opposite happened. It took constant corrections to make sure the aircraft stayed stable and on glide slope. In the Hornet, it was different. The two jet engines did not have P-factor, and both were essentially on the centerline of the aircraft. So even if one failed, it didn't create the yaw moment that the Hawkeye would experience. That being said, the Hornet had a faster approach speed behind the ship; therefore, things happened much quicker. Rattler found it was even more critical to keep his scan moving fast when he was flying the ball, or he would not notice the deviations that needed to be corrected.

Rattler began his turn to downwind when the radio came alive.

"Three-zero-five full stop this pass. Nice job tonight, Rattler," the LSO radioed. letting Rattler know he was done for the night and could full stop on centerline vice the carrier box on this next practice landing.

"Three-zero-five, copy all paddles," Rattler replied.

It had been a good night—one that Rattler needed to be prepared for the upcoming deployment. The squadron still had one more detachment on the USS *Stennis* before deploying a few months later. This would be a one-month detachment where the ship and air wing would get their final qualifications needed to be cleared to deploy. Rattler always wondered what would happen if they didn't get signed off. He hardly figured they would stop them from deploying. At any rate, that was well above his pay scale and not his problem. His job was to fly his aircraft and do everything he could do to be ready to deploy.

"Three-zero-five Hornet Ball, four-point-zero, Owen, full stop," Rattler radioed as his wings leveled and he started flying the ball.

"Roger, ball. Full stop," the LSO replied.

Meatball, lineup, and angle of attack were what was going through Rattler's mind as his hands made small corrections on the stick and throttles all the way to touchdown. The touchdown surprised him, and he almost added full power before realizing it was a full stop. He brought the throttles to idle and let the aircraft slow down to taxi speed. As he exited the runway, he dropped his mask, safed up his ejection seat, and went about the after-landing checklist items required prior to shutdown. The LSOs said they would debrief in the morning, so all Rattler had to do was fill out the flight time paperwork and head home. It would have been a great night to have Sandy waiting on him with a drink in hand, but that would have to be another night. Tonight, he would be greeted by a quiet house and an empty bed.

He sighed as he taxied into his parking spot and shut down the motors. Maybe the upcoming deployment would be good for him and keep his mind from thinking about her so much. *Just get through it, one day at a time*, he told himself as he climbed out of the jet and down the ladder to the dark ramp area. As he looked back up at the aircraft that he just flew, he still couldn't believe that regardless of all the things he had been through in the relatively brief career that had gotten him here, he was finally doing it. He was a fighter pilot.

Chapter Eight

"Thanks for doing this. I really appreciate it," Rattler said as he lifted the couch out of the back of his truck.

"No problem, brother," Maestro said. "I don't blame you one bit. If I was single, I would totally move my crap into storage before deployment. Unfortunately, with a huge family, I don't think they would be too happy about that."

Rattler laughed as he and Maestro continued to off-load the last of Rattler's possessions into a storage unit. He and the rest of the single officers would use one address while they were gone. This tended to be a common practice for people to save money while away. No reason to pay bills on a place you weren't going to be at for six to ten months.

"So, what are you going to do with all the money you'll bank from this?" Maestro asked.

"My goal is to get the old Shelby restored when we get back from deployment," Rattler replied.

"I was going to ask why you even keep that POS. It's in rough condition," Maestro said.

"I think it would be cool for my dad to see it back in all its glory." Rattler grinned.

The upcoming deployment was scheduled for six months, but Rattler knew better. Squadron life was going well, and he was getting his qualifications on schedule. The skipper definitely leaned on him on the officer side of things, tasking him with turning around the line division because the previous leadership really didn't do much. Rattler worked hard to set a new tone, and things were going well. The enlisted members of the squadron in the line division were some of the most junior, and therefore the most impressionable. Since Rattler took over, multiple people had been promoted, and one was selected for an officer program. Rattler was proud of that for sure.

The change of command was scheduled for the next day, and Rattler was put in charge of all the planning for that. Most of it was finished at this point, which gave him the opportunity to pack away his stuff before they left on deployment. He was scheduled to fly onto the USS *Stennis* one week from today, and that would be his new home. As he finished putting his belongings in the storage unit, with just enough room to fit everything around his '67 Shelby, he thought about the two regrets he had during this workup cycle. Due to the busy operational tempo and constantly being gone, he had not seen Sandy in over a month, and it had been even longer since he'd visited his parents. He had planned to fly a jet cross-county to go see them, but the weekend that was supposed to happen, the jet broke, and there just wasn't another opportunity. His dad took it in stride, but he could tell both his parents were pretty upset and had been looking forward to seeing him. He just hoped the deployment would go by quickly, and then he could spend some time with them. He even thought that if things kept going well with Sandy, maybe they could meet after this deployment.

Rattler closed and locked the storage unit and waved to Maestro, who was headed home to spend some time with the family. Rattler couldn't imagine what it would be like to leave for such a long time with a family at home. When he was in his E-2C Hawkeye squadron, he was married but didn't have any children. Maestro was a great guy, and the two of them had become close since Rattler joined the squadron. Rattler had a lot of respect for Maestro serving his country and showing his children why it was important to serve something bigger than yourself. It couldn't be easy, but Maestro did the best he could.

Rattler got into his truck and headed back toward base. He was scheduled to fly that evening and had to get ready. Basically, since he was living out of a suitcase at this point, it didn't really matter much what was going on during the day. He was preparing to deploy, and while he had been in this situation before, he knew it would be different this time. He was older and had more experience and knowledge of what to expect, but he would be on his own. Every time he launched on these deployments, success, failure, and often life or death would lay squarely on his shoulders. He just hoped he was up to the task.

CHAPTER NINE

"Okay, today is the day," Dice said in front of the ready room full of pilots. "Today we are hook down and heading west. Make no mistake that we will go into harm's way. While the Navy is inherently safer today than it was when I signed up, it is by no means a safe operation. You will be asked to push it over the next six months. There will be stresses at home and on the ship, and I need you to compartmentalize and do your jobs. Lives are at stake—those of your fellow squadron mates as well as the men and women on the ground. We are there to support them, and I expect you all to operate with the level of professionalism that has been formed in the history of naval aviation. We do not shy away from the threat. We run toward the sound of the gunfire and bring hell to our enemies. My goal is to bring everyone home safely and in one piece. If there are no questions, I'll see you on the ship."

The room was silent as the new skipper moved to the squadron duty officer's desk to check on the schedule. All the members of VFA-97 went about their business to get ready. Small bags had to be loaded into the jets, and final checks needed to be made. For most, if not all, of these pilots, this was the last time they would fly off of a land-based airport for months. The change of command had occurred a few days prior and went off without a problem. Both Professor and Dice were very happy, as were their families. Rattler couldn't help but notice that Professor was not happy to be leaving right before the action was about to start, but he seemed to have come to grips with the fact that he didn't have a choice.

Dice, on the other hand, was extremely excited to get this deployment started. Since he was a kid growing up around his fighter pilot father, he dreamed about taking his own squadron to sea and on a combat deployment. His speech at the change of command was filled with motivational catch phases to pump up his command, and it seemed to work. Professor and Dice couldn't be more different, and some in the squadron were excited about the change, while others didn't seem as happy.

"Rattler, you have any questions?" Toad asked.

"No, sir. I think I'm all set," Rattler replied.

"Yeah, have fun flying off the wing of the skipper," Toad said. "Just try to keep him out of trouble."

"You got it," Rattler replied as Toad walked out. It was clear to him that Toad and Professor had been closer, and Toad didn't feel the same love for Dice. Rattler figured what troubled Toad the most was that Dice would be writing his final FITREP and not the Professor. That gave him a lot of pull in either setting up Toad for future command or essentially ending his career.

Rattler, on the other hand, was doing great. As was normal during a change of command, the outgoing commanding officer had to write FITREPs for all the officers before he left. Professor wrote Rattler a top-notch one that put him well ahead of his peers. While some of the other junior officers weren't happy about Rattler jumping ahead of them, Rattler tried not to worry about it too much. Frankly, there wasn't anything he could do about it anyway. It was up to the skipper how he ranked everyone. But Professor had set Rattler up with his FITREP, and it was likely that Rattler would get selected for promotion to lieutenant commander soon and likely move on to a department head tour after he was done at the Warhawks.

"Let's do this!" Dice screamed to Rattler from across the room. "Are you pumped?"

"Yes, sir," Rattler replied.

"Okay, here is my brief," Dice said. "Be a good wingman, be in position, on time, and look good. Don't fuck it up. Questions?"

"No, sir." Rattler laughed as the skipper walked out of the ready room to get his flight gear on. While others were conducting a formal briefing on how to taxi out, join up, and fly to the ship for the first time in a long while, the new skipper essentially just high-fived his wingman and walked to the jet. He definitely had a different leadership style than Rattler had seen before, but you couldn't knock the old man's intensity or excitement.

Rattler walked downstairs to the hangar bay, which was mostly empty. The Warhawk jets had been staged on the flight line, and most of the crews that were launching the jets belonged to sister squadrons helping out. The vast majority of the Warhawks were already aboard the *Stennis*, and those that weren't were all staying behind on this deployment for various reasons. Rattler walked to a quiet end of the empty hangar and pulled out his phone. He made one last call. Earlier he had talked to his parents, and his dad told him he was proud of him and asked questions about how Rattler had prepped the Shelby for storage. His mother spoke very little. Rattler had seen this before and knew she was worried. Frankly, both his mom and dad were worried, but they dealt with it in different ways. Rattler had told them not to worry and that he would be home soon. Now it was time for one last call. He dialed Sandy's cell phone, which immediately went to voicemail.

"Hey, this is Sandy. Leave me a message," her voice said before a beep.

Rattler had thought about this a long time before calling, knowing that it would likely go to voicemail since she was flying on a trip around the globe.

"Hey, honey. It's Jack. Well, it's that time for real, I guess. I am about to walk to the jet and head out to the ship. I'll try to get my email set up as soon as I can and get in touch with you. Remember, no news is good news, and I will be fine. I miss you a ton. Honestly, when I met you that night in Dubai, I never would have thought that this relationship would grow. Thanks for always being there for me, and please stay safe. I love you and will call again soon." As Rattler ended the call, he saw the skipper walking proudly to his jet like a modern knight walking to his horse before a battle. Rattler couldn't help but wonder if all the sacrifice was worth it, but, ultimately, that didn't matter right now. He had a job to do, so he picked up his bag, checked his gear one last time, and shut his phone off. *Let's do this*, he thought.

CHAPTER TEN

BANG!

"Fuck!" Rattler mumbled as he woke with a start. The very first jets were launching, and he happened to be living right under the catapult, which made for a hell of an alarm clock. For a moment, he couldn't remember where the hell he was. Memories of his last Hawkeye deployment rushed into his head; and, for a moment, he thought he was in the six-man room on the *Nimitz*. He half waited to hear Clipper wake up or Ratbreath come in. But those days were over, and the room Rattler was in now was much smaller. He shared a two-man room with Maestro, which only happened because of dumb luck. At the very last minute, a member of the squadron had fallen and broken his leg, and it was clear that he wouldn't make deployment. The junior officer rooms were shuffled around, and Rattler and Maestro saw an opportunity to get into a two-man room and took it. It might not have made the other junior officers happy, but if it made Rattler's fourth deployment a little better, he didn't mind.

Rattler could tell quickly that the room was empty. His world came back into focus, and he remembered that Maestro was on duty today. Rattler took a moment to get his bearings and plan his day. Looking at his watch, he could see that it was 1300 local time, wherever the hell that was, and he knew he was scheduled for a night flight. He would be flying off the skipper's wing tonight and heading into country.

41

The deployment was going as well as could be expected; but, for the most part, it was quiet. Not too many pilots in the air wing were dropping bombs, and Rattler only had his hand at combat a few times himself. For the most part, it was very boring sitting on auto-pilot waiting for something to happen, which so far it hadn't. He knew better than to get complacent, though, because that was when naval aviation could kill you. Flying with the skipper was always a test in keeping his head on a swivel, and a nighttime combat mission would likely prove to bring some excitement.

Rattler got his things together and decided to grab a quick shower before getting some food. As he put on his shower shoes and grabbed his towel and shower bag, he checked to make sure he had his room key. Pretty embarrassing to get caught stuck out of your room after a shower. He made his way to the head and saw a sign that made him laugh. "Closed for cleaning." Of course, it was not the first, or likely the last, time he had been caught by that. No one was around, and he was tempted to go take a shower anyway, but he figured he better not. In today's Navy, there was probably a female enlisted sailor in there, and he would get court-martialed for going inside.

He made his way back to his room for a "bird bath" at the sink and then went up to the ready room. While he had been on the ship for a little over a month now and was settling into daily life, something in his gut had been nagging at him since he woke up. It was an uneasy feeling that he had felt before and had learned not to ignore. He still had to operate, but he recognized the feeling and kept his senses sharp to potential threats out there. He checked in his flight suit pocket for his dog tags and the cross that his aunt gave him; they were right where they were supposed to be. Stupid or not, that gave him the confidence that no matter what happened, he would be able to handle it.

Rattler reached the ready room of the Warhawks to find it very busy. Crews were briefing, and other pilots were checking emails in the corner. The ready room wasn't very big, but then again, the Warhawks had a lot less aircrew than the Wallbangers had. Being a single-seat Hornet squadron made for a lot fewer seats in the aircraft to occupy, and that suited Rattler just fine. He found Maestro behind the SDO desk, reading an email.

"Email from home?" Rattler asked.

"Yeah, man . . . just photos of the kiddos if they will ever download. How can we be on a nuclear-powered aircraft carrier and have such slow internet?" Maestro asked.

"Didn't you read that in the brochure when you signed up for the Navy? Want to see the world and have dial-up internet? Join us!" Rattler joked. "You ready to eat?"

"Yeah, I'll meet you in the wardroom. Let me just find someone to watch the desk while I eat," Maestro said.

"Okay, see you there," Rattler replied as he made his way out of the back door of the ready room and up to the forward wardroom. He couldn't help but notice that while the USS *Nimitz* and *Stennis* were essentially the same type and class of ship, they were so different. Little differences seemed like a big deal when you spent so much time at sea, but Rattler was adapting. Since the Warhawks were in one of the aft ready rooms, they rarely ate in the forward wardroom, but Maestro and Rattler liked to go up there to talk and get away from everyone. They shared common morals and values, and Rattler was happy to have made this connection after leaving the Hawkeye community.

After they ate, the day went by in the blur that was normal at sea. Rattler went about heading down to his division to check on his sailors and make sure they were handling life at sea okay. They had one of the hardest jobs on the flight deck day and night, and it could take its toll very quickly. Rattler was pleased to find that they were all doing well, and he felt like the division was coming along nicely. Afterward, he went back up to the ready room to check some emails. It seemed like every day was the same whenever he opened his inbox—a mix of work emails, emails from his parents, and a couple from Sandy.

She promised to write as much as possible and recently told him that she found writing helped her get through their time apart. She would often write emails on her breaks during her long international flights. She would always apologize for the ramblings, but Rattler loved them, not only because they made him feel connected to her, but because they also made him feel in touch with the real world. When you are on a ship at sea for a long time, it's easy to forget the real world, and Sandy was helping with that.

Of course, the photos of his hot Australian flight attendant in faraway lands didn't hurt his morale at all. When he was feeling lonely, she would always come through with a bikini picture from some beach layover she was on. She was working hard to save money in order to take some time off when Rattler got home. It was fun when she had a layover in Dubai or other parts of the world close to where the ship was operating. Of course, Rattler couldn't tell Sandy where he was, but he at least felt closer to her knowing she was near.

Before he knew it, it was time to suit up for his flight with the skipper. It almost seemed like a standard flight at this point. The two of them would be doing armed overwatch for a SEAL team on the ground in Afghanistan. Skipper was the lead, and Rattler would be his wingman. Toad had pulled duty of being the turning spare. Since combat ops were busy and the guys on the ground needed the airborne cover, it was not uncommon for someone to be the on deck or airborne spare. Sometimes, that meant launching with the rest of the aircraft, and when everyone checked in fully mission capable, you would just fly around and look for ships or whatever else the carrier wanted you to do. Other times, you were the turning spare, meaning you would preflight the jet and get it started, but not launch. If anyone had a problem, they would launch you to take their place. Rattler had done both, and he really didn't like either. At least airborne spare meant he got to fly, but he had a hard time getting his head in the game for a combat mission that he likely would not go on.

Tonight was different, and as Rattler sat in the mass brief and learned about the weather and who he and the skipper would be supporting, he had no problem keeping his head in the game. The skipper's excitement probably helped, as Rattler could feel the energy coming off the old man. This was what his whole life was built on, and every opportunity he had to do this job just made him more and more excited.

Rattler flipped through his various kneeboard mission cards, and he mentally thought his way through the flight, from the preflight to the launch and join up. They would then hit the tanker and head north into bad guy country. They would be in the threat envelope pretty much as soon as they went feet dry over land and stayed there until they returned to the feet wet, over the water, and back to the boat. While they had only left California a little over a month prior, the boat made a quick trip to the Indian Ocean, and this type of flight was becoming routine. This was evident in the briefs being shorter and most things being briefed as "standard."

Rattler looked around the room. Every aircraft was represented in this launch. All were doing different things, but Rattler saw crews from the Super Hornet, Prowler, and Hawkeye squadrons along with the pilots who would be flying the rescue helicopter, which seemed like it was always airborne. While each aircraft would launch on its own mission, it was interesting to see the difference in the crews. He saw the Hawkeye pilots in the back of the room looking like they were barely awake. Likely due to the operational tempo of flying so much and their lack of involvement in the mission, this brief was not very exciting to them. Rattler caught the eye of one of the Hawkeye pilots, who gave him a smile and a nod. The pilots of VAW-117 were mostly different from those who were there with Rattler, but they all knew of him. After Rattler's last deployment, CAG 11 had broken up, and squadrons went to different air wings, which seemed to be normal for today's Navy. Rattler never understood it, but in a weird stroke of luck, his old squadron would now be in CAG 9, which was where the Warhawks were assigned. It felt odd to Rattler sometimes, because flying the Hornet still felt like he was cheating on the Hawkeye.

The mass brief ended quickly, and each crew went back to their ready rooms to brief their individual missions for the night. Rattler, the skipper, and Toad went back to the Warhawk ready room, where the skipper quickly went through the brief and told Rattler he would see him airborne. As Rattler went over the mission in his mind, Toad sat down next to him.

"Everything going okay?" Toad asked.

"Yes, sir," Rattler replied.

"Come on, Rattler. You have been here for months. When are you going to drop the 'sir' stuff?" Toad asked.

"Well, to be honest, with the way things started with us and with your Naval Academy background, I just figured it was better to be formal," Rattler replied.

"Look, I was afraid of that. I am sorry for how things started with us. The news of losing Mike Maddox hit me hard, and then when I found out you two were in the same squadron, I took it out on you. I know deep down that you had nothing to do with Maddox's accident, and it was probably hard on you to lose a skipper and squadron mate. I have seen your work here, both in and out of the sky, and I'm impressed. Professor had a lot of respect for what he saw in you, and that showed in your FITREP. Frankly, I don't know if I have ever seen such a good FITREP for someone who hasn't been in the squadron for very long. I know you are trying to fit in around here, and I didn't make it any easier. I'm sorry for that, but please let your guard down a little around me. I can help you around here, and frankly, my wife loves Sandy and wants to hang out when we get home."

"Okay, I understand," Rattler replied, feeling awkward about knowing what really happened to CDR Maddox. "I'm still trying to get my feet under me here, but I appreciate your support."

"Good. Now do me a favor and make sure your jet is perfect because I could use a break tonight," Toad joked as he got up.

"You got it!" Rattler replied.

Rattler made his way to the PR shop to get his flight gear. After putting on his G suit, harness, and survival vest, he went back into the ready room to check out his 9mm pistol for the flight. Maestro was still at the SDO desk. From the look of things, he was still trying to download photos of his kids and was not any happier about the internet speed. From there, Rattler went to maintenance control to read the flight logbook for aircraft 304. Nothing really stood out to him, so before putting on his helmet, he signed for the jet and adjusted the fingertip light on his right hand. This light, which was a tiny LED light strapped to his index finger, would give him enough light to walk around the flight deck and also give him much-needed light in the cockpit to see his notes and kneeboard cards even while using his Night Vision Goggles. After this was complete, he walked outside the skin of the ship and onto the flight deck.

Rattler let his eyes adjust to the dark; and, immediately, his senses helped him see better. Even with his helmet on, he could hear everything from the aircraft being towed around to the flight deck chains that secured the planes down being carried. His nose was immediately assaulted by the smell of sweat, grease, jet fuel, and salty air. All of this, combined with his limited night vision, helped him find aircraft 304 on the bow of the *Stennis*. He approached and saluted the plane captain, a nineteen-year-old woman from his line division. Even under all her flight deck gear, her smile could not be hidden, as she was proud that her division officer was flying "her" jet that night. All of her preflight checks had been done, and the plane was ready.

Rattler made a quick walk around and climbed the ladder into the cockpit. Almost without thinking, his hands went about getting the aircraft ready for engine starts just in time for the 5MC to awaken the almost quiet on the flight deck. The air boss was announcing that flight ops would begin again and ended his speech with the command to start up the jets. A quiet, seemingly peaceful world immediately turned to full chaos as jets roared to life and maintenance personnel went about checking to ensure everything was in working order. Aircraft 304 seemed perfect, and Rattler gave the thumbs-up and closed the canopy. Outside, his plane captain handed the plane over to the yellow shirt on the flight deck, who immediately signaled to unchain the aircraft to ready it to taxi.

Watching the aircraft move around the flight deck was a sight to behold, as everyone had their job, and it all had to work together perfectly. To some, it might look like complete insanity, but to those in the know, it looked like an orchestrated masterpiece. Rattler made his way around the flight deck and then back up to catapult 2 on the bow. He looked over and saw a catapult weight board that matched the weight he had calculated for his aircraft at launch and gave a circle pattern with his fingertip light. This was his nighttime signal that he liked the weight, and the catapult officer would set the correct pressure to get Rattler and 304 airborne at the end of the catapult.

Time slowed as Rattler took it all in. It didn't matter how long he had been doing this job; nighttime operations never got too routine. The aircraft carrier was a dangerous place, and Rattler had a great deal of respect for it. Even in the middle of the craziness of night carrier operations, Rattler found times to calm down, take a look around, and take everything in. While sitting there on catapult 2, waiting to launch, he still had that nagging feeling in his gut. He recognized it, took a deep breath, and looked around the cockpit one more time. Everything seemed like it was in the right place. He reran his checklists from start to finish again to ensure he wasn't missing anything. Once he was satisfied that everything was okay, he put his head back and closed his eyes for a second. This gave him a chance to calm down and focus on the mission ahead.

Before he knew it, the catapult officer was giving Rattler the signal for launch. He put his left hand to full throttle and wiped out the controls with his right. Looking over his engines, everything appeared to be operating correctly, so he took a deep breath and flipped on his exterior lights with his left pinky, signaling to all on the flight deck he was ready to launch. He put his head back against the seat and waited for what always felt like an eternity before feeling the satisfying thump of the catapult steam releasing against the shuttle and his jet rocketing toward the end of the ship. Happy that all was good, he felt the end of the catapult and moved his hand down to the stick to begin to fly away. Just as he was doing so, everything went black.

CHAPTER ELEVEN

Time stopped as Rattler's brain went into hyper mode, trying to figure out what happened. He could not see anything inside the aircraft, and the pitch-black night didn't allow him to see anything outside. All he knew was that, a second ago, everything was working correctly, and now he wasn't sure if his plane was even flying. He also knew he didn't have any time to figure it out because he was only sixty feet off of the water. His left hand came off the throttles and moved to the ejection seat handle between his legs. He could almost feel the pain of the ejection, and it caused him to hesitate. Just like that, his brain snapped back into operate mode and his hand went back to the throttles and selected full afterburner, then gear up as his right hand pulled back on the stick.

He knew this was the moment of truth; the plane would either fly or it wouldn't. If it did, then he made the right decision not ejecting, but if it didn't, then he would likely hit the water any second, and it would be over. It felt like an eternity, but he could feel g-forces against his body, and his heart slowed down a little immediately. He was flying, which was good, but he still saw nothing in the cockpit to help him out. All his lights, displays, and electrical components were black.

It was strangely quiet, even though he was sitting just in front of two jet engines in full afterburner. He gazed outside to try to see which way was up, but he couldn't see the horizon since there was basically no moonlight. Emergency generators started up without him knowing it because his attention was 100 percent focused on trying to figure out where he was. Moments ago, he was on the flight deck of the USS *Stennis,* and then he was about sixty feet off the water. Now all he knew was that he was alive, for the moment, and could see nothing.

He had never seen a darker night as his eyes frantically tried to pick out anything outside to focus on. He briefly thought about putting on his Night Vision Goggles, but he decided against it since he was busy just trying to stay alive. His head's up display (HUD) was completely blank, and his standby gyro, which was extremely small and located down on the right lower side of his instrument display, was almost impossible to read. Without thinking, he put the stick in his left hand and shined his fingertip light at the standby gyro to see that he was approximately forty-five degrees nose up, assuming it was working correctly. If it was, he had to be climbing, so he pushed slightly on the stick to set twenty degrees up and switched the stick back to his right hand.

He looked outside again and could just slightly make out the horizon. If his eyes weren't lying to him, he was not anywhere near the water anymore, and for the time being, he was safe. He relaxed for just a second and felt happy to be alive. The respite was short-lived, as he realized he couldn't land on the ship like this or talk to anyone outside of his aircraft. Rattler felt very alone as he went about trying to get his electronics working again.

Troubleshooting with the pocket checklist was out of the question at the moment, as it was taking Rattler a lot of effort just to keep his wits about him. If he ended up in an unusual attitude, without the help of his flight instruments, he would likely have to eject anyway. So, he took his time. His flight school instructors talking about "no fast hands in the cockpit" came to mind as he slowly and purposely tried to get some instrumentation back online. He reached slowly to each display and cycled the power switch from on to off to on again and waited. He finished this with his HUD and allowed his eyes to focus outside.

His right display flickered to life, and just as Rattler let out a sigh of relief, it went blank again. His HUD was doing nothing, but then slower than normal, the left display came to life. Rattler began talking to himself, almost willing the plane to give him something to work with. He could land with one display. Although it was not something he wanted to do, it was possible. The left display reluctantly lit up, and the brightness was the most beautiful sight in the world. It looked like that display would be his only chance because nothing else came on. He methodically cycled through the pages on his display and finished on the attitude direction indicator (ADI). At least now he could see which way was up and which was down. He had no idea where the ship was, although it couldn't be too far away; but he needed to talk to someone outside of his plane.

Coming from a multicrew aircraft like the Hawkeye, it was unnerving to be so alone. Before he could begin working on getting the radios online, he looked up and, to his surprise, saw an aircraft right next to him. Although it startled him, it made him feel great. Like everything was going to be okay. The aircraft came very close, and he could see it was an F/A-18F Super Hornet from Rattler's sister squadron. The weapons systems officer (WSO) in the back seat began to send light signals to Rattler to get his attention. Rattler signaled back that he could not hear or talk on the radios, and the Super Hornet signaled they would take the lead of the formation. Rattler replied with a circle of his fingertip light that he acknowledged, and he went back to trying to cycle his radios on to off to on. He remained hopeful that he could talk to someone soon. Clearly, his combat mission was over, and he was not going to support the troops on the ground. His new war was to stay alive long enough to get back on the aircraft carrier in one piece.

Landing on an aircraft carrier, even in the best of conditions, was no small feat. Added to the fact that it was nighttime with zero moonlight, Rattler had very few instruments to rely on, and he couldn't talk to or hear anyone, and it would be damn near impossible. As he sat in his single-seat fighter aircraft, he realized he was holding his breath. He took a deep breath and let it out and almost laughed. He wondered how long he was holding his breath, but he forced himself to move in the seat and momentarily take his hands off the stick and throttles. He wiggled his toes in his size thirteen Redwing boots, trying to relax. It was a trick they taught pilots in flight school to relax while flying formation. If you kept too tight of a grip on the stick or throttles and you weren't relaxed, you would likely overfly the aircraft and make it harder to stay in position. Staying in position was critical tonight because the Super Hornet to his left was his only way back to the USS *Stennis*, which was the only place Rattler could land his plane. He continued trying to get either radio to work, but it didn't look like they were going to cooperate, so he finally gave up. He could technically land the plane in its current condition. While it wouldn't be easy, there were SOPs for situations like this.

He knew the Super Hornet he was flying off of was the event tanker and had been told that Rattler was in trouble. They probably worked with the ship and the E-2C Hawkeye airborne to get radar vectors toward Rattler before getting him on their radar. They didn't know what he was dealing with, so they had to initiate a join-up and hope that Rattler would not do anything erratic. Luckily for them, Rattler had no idea anyone was near him, and he just flew straight and as level as possible. Now that the formation was together, and they could give standard light signals, the Super Hornet would bring Rattler back to the ship and set him up to be fully configured with the landing gear, flaps, and arresting hook down, and about one mile behind the ship, they would "kiss off" Rattler and break away left and high. Rattler would then transition his scan from flying formation to flying the "ball" to landing. It would not be easy, but the LSOs would watch him. If he needed power, they would flash the green "cut" lights on the Fresnel lens, and if he was not in a safe position to land, they would wave him off. Rattler would execute the wave-off, and the Super Hornet would be in the correct position for Rattler to join back up and let them lead him back around the pattern to try again.

Of course, that was how it should work, but if they ever even remotely practiced anything similar, it was under more ideal circumstances and better weather, and certainly not with a broken Hornet with very few instruments to help the pilot fly. To put it in perspective, just losing the HUD was considered an emergency landing for a Hornet, and that was only one small part of what Rattler was dealing with. He remembered his training in the Hornet back in Virginia Beach, where senior instructors told him that being a good wingman was as important as anything else to a Hornet pilot, and right now Rattler understood why. He tried to focus on the important tasks ahead and not worry about the things he couldn't control. All he could do right now was stay in position and not lose sight of that Super Hornet. The sheer amount of focus this required his brain to use was likely strong enough to power some of his displays if only he could harness it.

Rattler continued to try to breathe and stay in a good position as the Super Hornet led him down toward the aircraft carrier. The silence was killing him as his brain continued to work in hyperdrive, trying to figure out what was wrong with his jet. Everything seemed so perfect on the flight deck, and then it all immediately changed, so Rattler couldn't help but think it was something he did wrong. Ultimately, there was nothing he could do at this point other than occasionally cycling the power on his radios in hopes that they would work, so he just concentrated on being a good wingman.

As the formation of jets descended toward the water, Rattler could sense they were slowing down. Almost on cue, the WSO in the back of the Super Hornet signaled that they were putting the flaps out and the arresting hook down. Rattler went about flipping the correct switches on his aircraft and hoped the systems would work. He had no way of knowing how far away from the ship they were or even what his configuration was. All he could do was trust his new flight lead and hope for the best.

It was at this point that he decided to do something that made him feel sick. While staying in formation, he reached with his right hand and unclipped his kneeboard from his right leg. There was no reason to have it on at this point, and it would only get in the way if he had to eject. He carefully stuffed it into his helmet bag and made sure that everything in the cockpit was secure. Now he was fairly confident that his jet was just having a massive electrical issue; and it was flying fine, but he also had no idea if that would change. If he had to get out of the aircraft quickly, he needed to be sure that nothing would injure him on the way out. Thinking about ejecting was something Rattler never liked. The idea of the seat crushing his spine with the force of twenty times that of gravity to get him away from the crippled jet, likely causing him to black out, only to then be floating down into the ocean at night was something he tried to force out of his head while sitting alone in aircraft 304.

Luckily, the next signal from his lead forced him to focus. The flight put their landing gears down, and Rattler knew they had to be close. He could feel the landing gear come down and the aircraft slow down even more. Focusing on the lead Super Hornet, Rattler saw a single light from the WSO make a circle, which he took to mean that Rattler's jet was okay to land. Unable to take it any longer, Rattler took his eyes off the lead jet momentarily to look forward and saw the lights of the aircraft carrier in the distance. He forced himself to look back at the lead, knowing for the next few minutes of his life, he would need to be at his best.

Time seemed to slow as Rattler kept in position and tried not to think about how hard flying the ball would be. Before he knew it, the Super Hornet flashed its exterior lights and then slowly broke away to the left. Rattler knew what that meant and gazed forward to see a familiar sight. Ahead lay the USS *Stennis*, sailing into the night. Rattler was on centerline and had just a slightly high ball on the Fresnel lens. Almost as soon as the connection from his flight lead left him, Rattler saw the "cut" lights on the lens from Paddles. It was a signal that the LSOs saw him, and he was cleared to land. Any future cut lights would mean Rattler needed to add power, and the wave-off lights would be the ultimate signal that he was not in a safe position to land.

Rattler kept his scan moving and focused as hard as he could. Time felt like it had stopped, but only once did he see a quick flash of the cut lights again, causing him to add a little power. Before he knew it, and to his surprise, he came crashing down onto the deck of *Stennis* and was immediately assaulted with his arresting hook catching a wire and bringing his jet from flying speed to a stop in less than one hundred feet. As the aircraft stopped in the landing area, Rattler moved his feet up onto the brake pedals, pulled the power to idle, and took a deep breath.

Signals from outside told him they were going to chain him to the deck right there and allow him to shut down. He relaxed for the first time since he had flicked on the exterior lights, telling the flight deck crew he was ready to launch, and he looked up through his canopy at the night sky. He saw the lead Super Hornet engage full afterburner and fly away into the night like an angel that was sent to keep him alive.

CHAPTER TWELVE

Rattler sat in the ready room chair, still in his flight gear, trying to process it all. He was happy to be alive, but he had no idea what could cause such a catastrophic loss of electrical power in his Hornet. Frankly, he was exhausted from the adrenaline dump, and those in the ready room gave him his space.

"Hey, Paddles!" Maestro said as the back door of the ready room opened.

Rattler stood because he knew they were here to talk to him, and he needed to hear his grade from the landing. As he turned around, he saw the LSO team, who all looked very tired. He didn't recognize any of them. He missed his days as an LSO and being part of the team, so he tried to muster a smile and walked toward the lead LSO.

"Hey, Paddles," Rattler said.

"Hey, buddy. Unreal night out there tonight, huh? Any idea what happened?" the lead LSO replied.

"No. Still waiting to hear from maintenance," Rattler replied.

"Okay. Well, three-zero-four, we had you little high come down all the way for the underlined OK three wire. Really nice job tonight," the LSO said.

"Thanks, Paddles," Rattler replied as the LSO turned around to leave. Rattler's landing had been unscheduled, and they needed to get back up to the platform for the next recovery. In typical naval aviation fashion, there was very little fanfare for doing your job, even if it was in extreme circumstances. After the LSOs left, Rattler looked at Maestro, shrugged, and left to get out of his flight gear. His night was over, and he would have to wait to see how the flight went with the skipper and Toad. Little of that concerned him now, as he just wanted to get out of his flight gear and grab a quick snack and shower. Fly, eat, sleep. Just another day on the aircraft carrier.

After grabbing a quick bite and a shower, Rattler was back at his desk in the two-man room checking his email. The room was actually designed for department heads, which meant that each desk had an internet connection. While this may seem like a simple thing, it made a big difference because it meant Rattler and Maestro didn't have to wait in line in the ready room to check emails. Rattler opened his laptop and connected to his email. The night was starting to wear on him, and he was getting tired, but he wanted to see if there was anything important he had to deal with before getting some sleep. Skipper wouldn't be back until much later, and he figured they would talk the next day about what happened. Hopefully, by then, the maintenance department could figure out what was wrong with the jet.

Rattler found the standard emails from the Navy and scanned them quickly so he could move on to the message from his parents. It looked like his dad had emailed to see how things were going on the ship and then gave a rundown on how things were going back home. All seemed good. Rattler could tell by the tone whether it was from his mom or dad, even though they shared an email account. This was clearly from his dad, and the email gave Rattler a good feeling that his parents were okay. Being disconnected from them his whole career had not been easy, and sometimes he second-guessed his career choice, but all things seemed to be going okay on the home front.

The last email was from Sandy, and as Rattler opened it, he was immediately transported to another place, not on an aircraft carrier.

Thoughts of his beautiful, blonde Australian girlfriend took him far away from everything he'd been through in the past couple of hours. He carefully read every word and then read it again. He didn't want to miss anything, because this connection was one of the few they had until he got off the ship. After rereading the email several times, he determined it seemed that Sandy was doing well and adapting to this long-distance, mostly email relationship just fine.

Rattler then did something he swore he wouldn't do. He hit reply and began to recount the sequence of events to Sandy. He knew as he was writing that it would be hard for her to read because she would worry about him, but Rattler needed to get it out, as he hoped it would help him get some sleep. As he wrote it, he didn't know if he would actually send it, but it was helping. He went over the feelings of uneasiness he experienced throughout the day, including how it felt to be back on the ship after it was all over. Writing about it helped him come to grips with how close he came to his own mortality, and he felt himself relax. He hit send and closed his laptop. Time to get some sleep. Tomorrow was another day, and he needed to be fresh for whatever this deployment would throw at him next.

The old man swiveled around in his huge leather chair to face his computer. He received a notification that the email he was waiting for had finally come. A smile crept over his face, and he logged into his computer. It was a smile of ego and power—one that only comes from the satisfaction of knowing that you are truly untouchable. Sure, this lieutenant in the Navy was completely insignificant to him and his world, but he wanted to know that he had the power to reach out and dictate anyone's fate, regardless of where they were in the world. Having that type of power makes you truly unstoppable.

His wrinkled fingers typed by pressing the keys of the keyboard one stroke at a time, indicating he never learned how to type correctly.

Little did that matter now in his life; anytime he needed something, he could just summon someone to do it for him. As he navigated through the various passwords and firewalls, the smoke from his Cuban cigar wafted into his nose. He had developed a taste for them on his first deployment out of the Academy and had a constant stash in the humidor at the other end of his office. Next to the cigar was the crystal glass of bourbon that sat untouched on his desk. He had to admit that recently the consumption of both had been accelerated as the stress of his plans coming together increased. He had plenty of money in offshore accounts to walk away right now and never want for anything, but like a drug addict, he wanted more. It was almost not as much about the money anymore as it was the power. He had new goals and new levels of control that whet his appetite, and he would not stop until he reached them. Although he would never run for public office, it wasn't because he didn't think he could win. Clearly, he had enough information on people to make any election a sure win, but since his Naval Academy days, he had learned that the person who actually sat in the office was just a pawn to someone else with the real control. He wanted to be the person in control, hiding in the dark, pulling the strings and controlling the agenda.

He opened his inbox to see a single email with no subject. His obsessive-compulsive side ensured that even on this completely secure account, every email was filed in the proper place and out of sight when the main screen was displayed. He learned long ago that you can never be too careful when it came to security. This was evidenced by the second computer screen on his desk, which constantly monitored the thirty-six cameras that surrounded his private property. A squirrel couldn't take a piss on his acreage without him knowing it. Satisfied by his soon-to-be confirmed triumph, the old man took one more long pull from his Cuban cigar, then picked up the crystal glass of bourbon and took a sip as he clicked open the email.

"Operation Snake Bite . . . Failure," flashed across his screen. With rage, the old man threw the crystal against the wall and slammed his fist into the desk in a thundering clap.

CHAPTER THIRTEEN

"Do you ever worry about your luck running out?" Sandy asked after taking a sip from her glass of wine.

"Wow, that's a hell of a question." Rattler laughed. The *Stennis* had pulled into port in Dubai the day prior, and Sandy was able to work her schedule to be there at the same time. From the minute Rattler saw her, he could tell she was tired. She was working very hard to fly as much as possible, not only so she could take time off when Rattler's deployment was over, but also to keep her mind off him being away. After dinner, they were finishing up some wine at a restaurant when she asked Rattler to tell her firsthand the story of his Hornet going completely dark off the catapult shot. While Rattler really didn't want to relive that night, he also knew that it was important for Sandy to understand it. He had unloaded on her in an email, mostly because he needed to talk to someone. Unfortunately, email is a one-sided conversation, and it left her with more questions than answers. She loved that he was safe, but she wondered how much time he had before his luck would run out.

"Maybe it's all skill and not luck," Rattler joked.

"Okay, cowboy. But seriously, do you worry when you are up there?" Sandy asked again.

"Sorry. Didn't mean to make light of your question. But the answer is mostly no. I have learned to just listen to my gut and try to do the best I can. When it comes to nights like that, there is no time to worry. Honestly, I was so far behind that jet that I was lucky to fly away from the water. You can't worry about that, though. I know it sounds weird, but could you imagine if you were always worried about crashing on every flight you worked? You would never go to work. I guess that's how it is with me. I've heard stories of guys hanging it up and not being able to handle it. I hope to retire or move on to something else before I get to that point—kind of walk away in my prime. I don't want to be forced out or be like an old football player still suiting up well past when I should have left," Rattler replied.

"You going to fly the friendly skies?" Sandy joked with a wink.

"I've never given much thought to what I would do after this, honestly. I mean, I don't come from an aviation background. Years ago, I figured I would have kids and settle down, but that didn't pan out the way I thought it would. Maybe the airlines would be the next step. I heard they make decent money and have a good schedule, but I would have to do a lot of research before I made that jump," Rattler replied.

"I'm not sure you'd like flying all over the world with sexy flight attendants bringing you snacks and talking your ear off," Sandy teased.

"You don't think I'd like that, or you wouldn't like me doing that?" Rattler joked back.

"Guilty!" Sandy smiled. "How are you fitting in with your new squadron?"

"I think it's going pretty well. Maestro is definitely a good friend now, and I'm happy that our paths crossed, but overall, everyone is pretty cool. It's just different from the Wallbangers. Maybe it's because we are all so damn busy, or maybe it's something else, but it just feels different. Maybe that will change once I'm here a little longer." Rattler took another sip of wine and thought about how things had been going.

Overall, pretty good, he thought. Definitely not the close connections that he had in his previous squadron, but that was to be expected. He was older and more experienced now, and with that came different priorities. He was working hard to make the next milestones in his career, and he was not the same age as the twenty-four-year-old junior officers who were just checking in. He was also younger than the department heads and the skipper and XO, so he was kind of in no-man's-land. Maestro was the same age as Rattler since he joined the Navy a little later than most. He had done a few jobs in the music industry prior to going to Officer Candidate School, and maybe it was those life experiences that enabled them to get along so much. Rattler was deep in thought when Sandy interrupted.

"Another bottle for the room, honey?" Sandy asked again.

Rattler looked up at the waiter, who was waiting for his answer and was clearly not impressed with Rattler's daydreams.

"Yes, I think so," Rattler replied. "Sorry about that."

"No problem. It's getting late, and I would like to slip into something more comfortable," she replied as she stood to head up to their hotel room.

Rattler grabbed the bottle of wine and followed Sandy to their room. As they waited for the elevator, he watched pilots from the air wing running around the hotel and could only laugh at the memories he had of Clipper and their adventures in the past. Maybe what they say about your first squadron being special and no other squadron being the same was true.

As they rode the elevator to their floor, Rattler was taken aback by Sandy's beauty again. It would be one thing if she was just beautiful, but there was something else about her that made her even more radiant. Maybe it was her personality or her sense of humor, but the woman standing across from him was the most beautiful sight he had ever seen, and he wasn't about to miss one second with her in this port. As they walked to the room, Rattler held her hand, and when they approached, he opened the door and let her in. She squeezed his hand slightly as the door shut behind them, and then she let go. Rattler stood, waiting to see what she was doing, as she walked back to the door, grabbed the "do not disturb" sign, opened the door, and hung it outside with a wink. It was good to be off the ship with the woman he loved.

CHAPTER FOURTEEN

The black SUV came to a stop at the end of the long gravel driveway. The man driving clearly had been here before, but this was the passenger's first time. He was nervous as he reached for the door handle and got out. Pebbles crunched under the soles of his expensive, civilian-version combat boot knockoff. He looked the part and was trying to convince himself that he was ready to enter this world. The two walked up to the front door of what could only be described as a mansion, and the door opened to greet them. Without a word, a doorman of sorts escorted them through the house and to the back office. When the office door opened, they could see an old man sitting at his desk. He motioned for both men to sit, and the doorman left the three alone. Without giving them a second to think, the old man began.

"Operation Snake Bite was a failure. I want to make one thing very VERY clear. I do not fail!" The old man stood from behind his desk. What he lacked in stature, he made up for in confidence. "I have worked my whole life for what you see here, for the future of myself and my family. I will not have some hotshot fighter pilot wannabe messing that up. He has somehow gotten himself into this, and we are going to take care of that. We have tried multiple times to get rid of him, but now I'm changing my plan. That is where you two come in." The man reached into his desk and pulled out a file. He slid it across his desk and continued. "If I cannot get to the man, I will go after the thing he loves."

The two men opened the file to see photos of a beautiful woman. Her long blonde hair and electric smile stood out as they flipped through the documents. They saw her comfortable at home, then in her flight attendant uniform at work, and finally with Rattler during their latest time together. Both men scanned the photos without a word while the old man continued. "This is Rattler's girlfriend, Sandy; you will find her and take care of her. I want it to look like an accident, but only to a point. I want this young man to question what he has gotten himself into and hopefully stop what he is doing and leave us to our plan. If you fail, this will be the last time we work together. Do I make myself clear?" the old man asked as he looked up from his desk.

His question was met with no words but two simple head nods. This was why he liked working with individuals like them. They were simple men who didn't think too much. They were the muscle he lacked naturally, and while he needed them, they were replaceable. "Good. That is all," he finished as the door opened and the doorman appeared to escort the men out.

With the men gone and the door closed again, he leaned back in his chair. His mind wandered to thoughts of his family and how he had gotten to this point in life. As a man, he felt like he had accomplished everything, but he was all alone. Those around him only feared him, and that is why they obeyed. He told himself that he did it all for his family, but the truth was he rarely ever saw his family anymore. While he had provided them with everything they could possibly want, it hadn't stopped them from using him and moving on. His wife of a lifetime had passed from cancer years before, and their children had started their own lives. Their futures would be taken care of, but for a man who once did everything for the greater good, even he could see how he had changed. It had become about ego now and being in control. This world had taken everything that mattered to him, and he wanted that power back.

Over the years, he had gotten closer until some Navy pilot stuck his nose in where it didn't belong. Now the fight was back for the old man. It was personal again, and he felt more alive than he had in many years. He was in control now and would not lose. He closed his eyes, and visions of his wife entered his mind. A smile crept across his face, and he let out a huge breath. The fate of another human had been sealed, and the hunt was on . . . He was back in control.

CHAPTER FIFTEEN

The plan was simple. Rattler was out of night currency on the ship and needed a day landing before he could fly again at night. His last flight before the port call did not go as planned, and while he had gotten a night trap, he also hadn't flown for a few days prior to entering port. His skipper assured him they would get him qualified after port and not to worry about it. Today was the day. A simple single-cycle hour flight by himself with no real mission other than to get a day landing. Then he would brief to be the mission spare tonight for another combat mission. He likely would not go, but he would be an airborne spare, so he would ensure he got his night trap. *Back to life at sea*, Rattler thought as he did the preflight walk around of his F/A-18C Hornet.

His Hornet sat on the bow of the carrier in the sunshine as he approached it. The sounds and smells of the flight deck filled his senses immediately. There wasn't a cloud in the sky, and the sun, although very warm, painted a beautiful picture on the flight deck that only a naval aviator could appreciate. Rows upon rows of fighter aircraft loaded with bombs and missiles, which are ready to do God's work to protect the men and women on the ground, along with support aircraft scattered around. The helicopter was turning on the port side of the ship and changing aircrew, readying to launch again. Rattler had a lot of respect for the crews of those aircraft. He never wanted to fly helicopters, but it had more to do with the safety aspects of it versus the mission. Airborne search and rescue were immensely important, and while it was never said, every aviator went airborne, knowing those helicopter crews were ready to pluck them out of the water if needed. Additionally, if they went down behind enemy lines, they knew someone would come to get them. It was that trust and bond that allowed Rattler and the others to do their job, day in and day out.

He approached the Hornet like an old friend. While it had only been a little over a week since he had flown, it felt like much longer. The malfunction flight, followed by his time in port with Sandy, had distracted his mind from the routine of the ship. Routines were the key to keeping this job as safe as possible, and Rattler found himself falling back into his routine almost immediately. He stepped around the aircraft, running his gloved hands over certain parts of the plane like he had been taught to do in training and had done on every flight since. Once satisfied that the aircraft was in top shape, he climbed the boarding ladder, placed his tapes in the tape recorder behind his seat, inspected the ejection seat to ensure it was in the "safe" position, and then climbed in. Even strapping into the jet was routine as he started with his leftmost lap belt and worked clockwise until he had everything strapped to his survival harness. Then, without thinking, his hands went to work on the interior preflight and getting the jet set up and ready to start the engines.

At that point, he had a moment to stop and take in his surroundings. On an aircraft carrier, rarely do you start the engines until you are told to. He wanted to be completely ready to crank the massive afterburning engines of the Hornet as soon as the air boss gave permission, but he had some time now. He looked down at the Breitling watch his parents had given him as a gift for getting his wings, and he saw he had five minutes to himself before engine starts.

Looking at the watch made him smile as it brought back memories of his parents—two hard-working, middle-class people who always provided for Rattler and his older sister. They owned an auto mechanic shop and worked day in and day out in the family business. While it was stressful at the time, it had shown Rattler and his sister the value of both hard work and the importance of family. The cost of this watch must have taken his parents quite some time to save for as well as hard work getting extra business to pay for it, and because of that, Rattler always wore it. In a weird way, it made him feel closer to his parents, even far away in the middle of an ocean with no land in sight. Memories of his childhood and family were abruptly cut short when the air boss came on the 5MC, announcing the start of the launch. He told everyone on the flight deck that didn't need to be there to exit and then gave the pilots permission to start the engines.

Rattler didn't have a conscience thought as his hands moved around the cockpit of the Hornet, starting the engines and getting the mission computers online and ready for flight. Before long, he was closing the canopy and signaling that he was ready to taxi. Since he was ready relatively quickly, and since his mission was quite benign, he taxied aft from the bow to the stern of the ship and turned around. While keeping one eye on the yellow shirt that was giving him taxi instructions, he watched the other aircraft get ready for launch. While turning on the stern, he saw the LSOs preparing to recover the airborne aircraft after the launch was complete. He gave them a thumbs-up and received the same as he taxied by.

While he was not actively waving aircraft anymore in his Hornet squadron, he was an LSO and tried to get up to the platform when he could just to hang out. He missed the comradery of being on the team. Next up was seeing the weight board and giving a thumbs-up that it matched his calculation of the requirement to get his heavy Hornet airborne at the end of the catapult. This was followed by being handed off to another yellow shirt whose job was to taxi to the catapult. Behind Rattler, the jet blast deflector rose to protect those around him from his jet blast when he went to full power on launch.

Time passed quickly while Rattler waited on catapult 4 for launch. The yellow shirts worked hard to position aircraft for the launch and then be ready to clear the landing area for the airborne aircraft to come aboard. If executed correctly, they would have forty-five seconds from the last aircraft launching off the waist catapults before the first one landed. They did this day in and day out, twelve or more times a day. It became a beautiful masterpiece of chaos.

Before long, Rattler was handed off to the shooter, who was likely a P-3 pilot on his disassociated sea tour. His job was to launch the aircraft day and night. Today, the shooter was on deck, but they could also do their job from the bubble, which was a type of mini office that would raise up out of the flight deck in bad weather. The shooter gave Rattler the signal, and Rattler went to full power with his left hand while wiping out the controls with his right hand and cycling the rudder pedals with his feet. His eyes quickly scanned the engine and systems pages to ensure the Hornet was ready for flight.

Once Rattler saluted, there was little that could be done to stop the launch. Satisfied that the aircraft was ready, Rattler saluted with his right hand, put his head back against the ejection seat's headrest, and put his right hand on the "towel rack" handle on the right side of the canopy bow. Hornet pilots did not hold the control stick during launch because the computers of the Hornet would program the proper amount of nose up at the end of the catapult to get flying. Having their hand on the stick could cause the pilot to actually pull back when it was not needed, which could cause the plane to stall immediately when airborne.

Rattler waited while the shooter checked to ensure everything was ready and safe, and then he reached down and touched the deck. That was the signal for the final step. A young, enlisted woman to the left of Rattler's aircraft stood at a panel next to the flight deck with her hands in the air. She saw the signal from the shooter, and she looked forward and aft one last time to ensure the path was clear; then her right hand came down and pushed a red button. With that, Rattler and his Hornet rocketed down the catapult, reaching a speed of over 180 mph in less than two seconds, and he was flying. He immediately took a little check turn to the left to clear the path of any planes launching off the bow; then he picked up his landing gear and shook off the adrenaline of the best roller-coaster ride he could imagine.

With this being a case one launch, Rattler didn't have to talk to anyone. He liked it that way. He could just fly and get away from the ship before checking in with Red Crown, the destroyer that would act as air traffic control, checking aircraft in and out as they left and returned to the ship. Since this flight was really to get Rattler a day trap, he didn't expect too much from Red Crown when he checked in. Rattler was fragged to get a little gas from an airborne Super Hornet, and after heading above the ship to the tanking altitude, he made his way away from the ship. He cycled to button four, which was Red Crown, and checked in.

"Red Crown, three-zero-one outbound for checks," Rattler radioed.

"Three-zero-one, Red Crown. We have you sweet, sweet. Standby for immediate tasking," Red Crown replied.

Rattler tensed immediately. He was expecting the "sweet, sweet" call because that was Red Crown's way of telling him his systems were reporting his position correctly, but the "immediate tasking part" surprised him. He didn't have to wait long to find out that his easy day flight was about to change.

"Three-zero-one contact BRAA 360/75 angels ten. Aircraft six-one-one is in trouble . . . buster!" Red Crown replied.

Without thinking, Rattler pulled the jet's nose around to the heading Red Crown had given as his left hand selected full afterburner. Aircraft 601 was the airborne Hawkeye, and they were experiencing problems. Rattler wasn't going to wait around to find out more. He looked at his fuel gauge while he worked his radar to get a lock onto the Hawkeye. He had work to do.

CHAPTER SIXTEEN

Rattler pulled the power back slightly as he reached the best speed for his Hornet to close the distance between him and the Hawkeye. He had not been able to get the Hawkeye on the radio, but Red Crown had told him they had radioed a Mayday call and were experiencing engine problems. Rattler checked the air plan that was on his right kneeboard and saw that the plane was on its way back from a combat mission. They had been airborne for a long time and likely didn't have a lot of fuel to play with. He also knew from his experience flying the Hawkeye that it could fly on one motor with little issues, so that left him with more questions than answers. All he could do now was join up on the stricken Hawkeye and hope to get the pilot on the radio.

His hands worked the buttons on the stick, throttles, and radar while he tried to get a lock on what he thought was the Hawkeye based on the vectors that Red Crown had given him. Finally, as he cursed the Hornet, the radar took a lock. Rattler could tell it was the Hawkeye based on the readout in his HUD and also his right digital display indicator (DDI). Now it was time to make this join-up happen. "Red Crown, what frequency is six-zero-one up?" Rattler asked on button four.

"Three-zero-one, we are comm out with them at the moment," Red Crown replied.

Rattler felt the frustration of a mission not going as planned, and he told Red Crown that he would be off frequency for a moment and was radar locked on the Hawkeye. He went about cycling through all the logical frequencies that the Hawkeye might be up based on where they were and the weather they were flying in. At least it was a beautiful day, which would help. He pulled the power back a bit more as he worked on the geometry for the join-up. He tried to stay aware of how much fuel he was using. There was also a balance between getting a mission like this done and running low on gas. The F/A-18C aircraft was not known for being able to carry a lot of extra gas. The configuration Rattler was flying was what the pilots called "double ugly," which was their normal combat load. He would have normally had a laser-guided five-hundred-pound bomb, a five-hundred-pound Joint Direct Attack Munition (JDAM), and two drop tanks that could hold about two thousand pounds of external fuel. One was mounted directly beneath the centerline of the aircraft, and the other was mounted under his wing, hence the double ugly nickname. It didn't make for the sexiest-looking aircraft, but it gave Rattler the extra gas he needed to get the job done. Additionally, Rattler was happy to have the ability to get extra gas while flying. Although he was not scheduled to get any today, he knew that if something went really wrong, the ship would launch extra tanker aircraft to help out. That was a luxury he never had when he was flying the Hawkeye.

Last on the list of things that Rattler liked about flying the Hornet compared to the Hawkeye was the ejection seat he was sitting on. It was no more or less comfortable than the seat in the Hawkeye, but the ability to get out of the aircraft quickly if needed put him at ease. He was hoping he could go his whole career without having to use one, but better to have it and not use it than the other way around. Rattler briefly remembered the insanely complicated way they were trained to bail out of the Hawkeye, which involved getting out of the seat with your parachute attached and walking down a narrow corridor from the cockpit to the main entrance, where you just jumped and then deployed your parachute. Not an option Rattler ever wanted to experience.

Rattler moved his scan more outside now. He had been working the join-up geometry almost solely on his radar display with the autopilot on to ensure he could focus up to this point, but he knew he was getting close and needed to scan his surroundings to visually pick up the Hawkeye so he could join quickly and efficiently and provide whatever help he could. The fact that they weren't talking to anyone concerned him a bit. As much as Rattler loved to give naval flight officers (NFOs) a hard time, there were three in the back of that Hawkeye with more radios than they could possibly use at once. Not being able to reach the Hawkeye on any radio at all was not normal. Rattler hoped that once he joined on the plane, he could use old-fashioned hand signals to get the pilots' attention and help them back to the ship.

If he had been paying closer attention to the target in his HUD, he would have seen that the Hawkeye was slowly but steadily losing altitude. This could be written off to the crew trying to get in position to land on the ship, but it could also indicate much more. It almost startled Rattler when the Hawkeye came into view because it definitely didn't look normal. He picked up the Hawkeye at fifteen miles about his ten o'clock relative, and within a few seconds, he noticed that while the right motor seemed to be working fine, the left propeller was windmilling and not feathered. Additionally, there was a trail of smoke behind the left motor.

Rattler's mind immediately started racing. The left motor of the Hawkeye was considered the critical engine, meaning that because both propellers turned in the same direction, the P-factor of the aircraft was turning to the right or clockwise from the perspective of the pilot flying the plane. Therefore, if you shut down the left motor, it was harder to fly the plane than if you shut down the right motor. The aircraft was in a slow, steady descent, and every-thing became clear to Rattler in an instant. The left motor was not feathered, meaning it was providing drag. The Hawkeye could fly on either single motor, assuming the dead engine was feathered. If it was not, it would provide too much drag to allow the aircraft to hold level flight. Aircraft 601 was not in a steady descent to land on the ship; it couldn't hold altitude, and the crew would either have to bail out or ditch the aircraft.

CHAPTER SEVENTEEN

"Red Crown, this is three-zero-one. Launch the SAR helo. I repeat LAUNCH THE SAR HELO onto my position. Six-zero-one is an emergency aircraft, left motor failed and not feathered, cannot hold level flight," Rattler radioed over button four.

The controller on the other end of the radio immediately jumped into action. He was only twenty-two years old, but he had been trained for this. His hands were switching radios and alerting the proper chain of command to the call Rattler had just made. He had never met Rattler in person and likely never would. They were deployed on two different ships that just happened to work together in the same battle group. Their lives would forever be connected based on that radio call, and the actions that came in the next few seconds could mean the difference between life and death for the crew of 601.

On the flight deck, the helicopter that had just landed was immediately jumping into action. Prior to the launch, the oncoming helo launched with a mission of basic plane guard, as the pilots called it. They would hang out around the carrier, ready to jump into action if something happened on either the launch or recovery. This was their standard day, and while they briefed contingencies, it all seemed very mundane. The helo that landed was being towed away from the landing area. The crew immediately started getting the aircraft ready to launch again, and a new crew was readying themselves below decks. They would be airborne again in a matter of minutes.

If you happened to be standing on the flight deck during this, you would not have noticed anything out of the ordinary. Shipboard operations were a controlled chaos all the time, so the slight differences would not stand out at all. Additionally, if you had looked up, you likely would not have noticed that the Super Hornet tanker circling at five thousand feet above the ship had just joined back up with the off-going tanker to take on more gas. The air boss was assembling his assets to use them the best he could while more assets were getting ready on the flight deck. Below in ready room 8, the phone rang, and as the SDO answered, he heard a one-way conversation. It was CAG telling him to get a pilot and another tanker airborne NOW! Again, complete coordinated chaos, but like typical naval aviation, it all worked out . . . usually.

Not much of those details mattered to Rattler in his single-seat Hornet, which was now flying off the left wing of Hawkeye 601. As he stabilized himself, he saw that the Hawkeye was established in an eight hundred feet per minute rate of descent, give or take. It didn't take Rattler long to figure out that they would run out of altitude long before they made it to the ship. Without thinking, he flew his aircraft loosely off the side of the Hawkeye to ensure the pilot had enough room to maneuver. Reaching into his helmet bag tucked in on the ride side of the Hornet cockpit behind his right arm, he pulled out a checklist he hoped he would never need. Keeping his cross-check focused on both the Hawkeye and his own flying, as well as monitoring his systems, he opened up the checklist to the "Search and Rescue (SAR)" on-scene commander section. He briefly scanned what he needed to do in the event the Hawkeye crew had to bail out or, worst case, ditch the aircraft. He knew that other assets would be overhead quickly to relieve him, but he didn't want to screw this up. He had practiced this in the Hawkeye many times in training when he was assigned to VAW-117 prior to getting the transition to fly F/A-18s, but this time was different for two reasons. First, he was alone in his aircraft with no one to back him up, and second, there were real lives at stake. This wasn't some training mission derived from his leadership to test his skills.

Rattler knew what he had to do and moved his aircraft forward to try to get the attention of the pilot in the left seat of the Hawkeye. He could quickly tell that the pilot was busy trying to fly the aircraft. Rattler couldn't get over seeing the left motor just windmilling out there. He knew that was bad. At times like this, his thoughts would often drift back to his past. His uncle once said it was his brain's way of protecting him, slowing things down so he didn't make quick decisions that he would regret. He told him stories of Vietnam when the same thing would happen to him.

In his mind, Rattler drifted back to his training in the Hawkeye years before and remembered they focused a lot on getting the propeller feathered quickly. He didn't think that the Hawkeye was flyable in the current situation, and it didn't look good. Rattler considered crossing under to the right side of the aircraft to see if the copilot might notice him. About the time he was pulling the power back to drift aft and pass behind the Hawkeye, Rattler saw something that caused his heart to sink.

In aircraft 601, the junior NFO in the back was first to the door. The radar officer sat in the forward most seat in the aft of the aircraft and was primarily responsible for getting the radar up and running at the start of the flight and then monitoring the radar for the duration of the mission. It was a critical and time-consuming job that ultimately could mean the difference between the other two NFOs having a good radar picture or not. Also, by sitting further forward, he was the first to get to the exit door. With very little being said after the aircraft commander made the bail-out call over the internal communication system (ICS), this first-tour NFO stood in the middle of the stricken Hawkeye, looking at the jettison handle. This situation was the focus of training at the fleet replenishment squadron of VAW-120 and was constantly retested throughout his time in the fleet. The idea was that if you ever found yourself in a situation where you had to "blow" the door, you didn't have time to think. You just had to fall back on your training and know what to do.

The E-2C Hawkeye was a relatively safe aircraft. It was built by Grumman Iron Works, and variations of the current Hawkeye have been flying since the 1950s. Even during that length of time, there were relatively few mishaps. These aircraft had redundant systems that helped mitigate the risks, and while they did not have ejection seats, due to the fact that the NFOs sat directly under the giant radar dome, the crew did have the ability to bail out of the aircraft. On every flight, each crew member would strap the survival vest to the seat they were assigned to sit in for that mission. On the back of that seat was a parachute that, if needed, would unhook from the seat base and go with the crew member as they walked to the exit door to bail out. While the corridor between the cockpit and the aft of the plane was narrow, it was possible for the aircrew—either pilot or NFO—to essentially get up, walk to the door, and jump.

On paper, it sounded like a great backup plan, but in practice, there were only a few examples of crews actually trying to do it. During his days flying the Hawkeye, Rattler always wondered where the door would go, and if it would hit the tail when it came off the aircraft. Now fast-forward many years later, he was sitting in a Hornet and his question got answered. The door came off the Hawkeye cleanly and fell down and aft, then quickly out of sight. Rattler didn't think to mark his location in case the Navy wanted to recover the door, but that was the least of his concerns when he saw the first NFO approach the exit door.

CHAPTER EIGHTEEN

The flight of the Hornet and the Hawkeye was only about four thousand feet over the water when the first NFO jumped. Rattler craned his head back to keep the guy in sight, all while flying off the left wing of the Hawkeye and trying to keep a decent distance in case the pilot needed to maneuver the aircraft. He had been flying next to the plane for what felt like forever now, but in reality, it was under ten minutes. He had never been able to reach any of the aircraft on the radio and essentially just had a front-row seat to this mishap.

About the time Rattler lost sight of the crew member who jumped, he saw a parachute. For a moment he relaxed, knowing that at least one crew member had escaped, but there were four to go.

"Red Crown, three-zero-one, mark my position. Six-zero-one is bailing out right now. I have one, no make that two good parachutes," Rattler said as he noticed the second parachute deploy quickly, followed by the third person at the door. Without hesitation, the crew member jumped and must have immediately pulled the ripcord, because, from Rattler's vantage point, it seemed like the parachute opened very close to the tail of the Hawkeye. That was three aircrew out and two to go.

Rattler relayed this to Red Crown to coordinate SAR assets, all while flying and starting the SAR on-scene commander checklist. At the same time, Rattler saw the fourth crew member come to the door. Rattler had to fly slightly lower than the Hawkeye on the left side to keep the door in sight, and now they were getting low enough that he made a mental note to watch his altitude. No use flying his own aircraft into the water. He reached up and set his radar altimeter bug to five hundred feet, so it would warn him to pull up if he got that low.

Looking back at the Hawkeye, he saw the crew member was still standing at the door. He seemed to hesitate and didn't want to jump. At one point, Rattler saw him look back toward the cockpit before looking out of the exit door again. As they passed through two thousand feet above the ocean, the pilot seemed to take one more look and then jumped. Moments later, the parachute deployed, and Rattler marked the position.

His easy day flight had quickly become anything but that, but he had now watched four aircrew successfully bail out of a Hawkeye. He just needed the last pilot to get out, and then, hopefully, the helicopter would be along shortly to pick them up. Looking out of his aircraft, the sea seemed fairly calm, and the weather was beautiful, so Rattler figured the helicopter pilots would be able to find them quickly. They were now less than fifty miles to the aircraft carrier, and while Rattler didn't know much about helicopters, he knew they would be here shortly.

Rattler was waiting for the last pilot to get out of the aircraft but could still see him in the cockpit flying the aircraft. It didn't make sense. Everyone else was out. Rattler pushed the throttles up slightly and closed the gap between the Hawkeye and his Hornet. He wanted to be careful because he still wasn't sure the Hawkeye pilot even knew he was there. As he approached, he moved forward to try to get the pilot's attention. In the Hawkeye, the pilot was looking forward, and Rattler could sense his concentration. Rattler briefly thought about trying to fly in front of the Hawkeye to get his attention, but then he realized they were passing through a thousand feet above the ocean and there wouldn't be time to join back up. Rattler was about to give up when the pilot looked over. In a brief moment, the two pilots were connected. The Hawkeye pilot gave Rattler a thumbs-up. Rattler replied with the same. While he was trying to figure out how to signal the Hawkeye pilot to bail out, he got his reply. The Hawkeye pilot took a long look at Rattler, their gazes frozen in time. The Hawkeye pilot tapped his helmet and then pointed at the water. For a second, Rattler was confused, and then it all became clear. The only reason the Hawkeye was flying in a controlled manner was because of that pilot.

After over one thousand hours flying the Hawkeye, Rattler was surprised how he forgot certain things very quickly. He was so used to flying the Hornet with its advanced systems that he forgot that the Hawkeye had a very basic autopilot. Many times, the Hawkeye autopilot would not work at all. Rattler had flown plenty of six-hour flights in the Hawkeye, where he had to "hand fly" the whole time with no pilot relief. Rattler soon realized that the pilot could not bail out because no matter how well he trimmed up the aircraft, as soon as he let go of the controls, it would not stay straight and level long enough for him to bail out. He was going to ditch the aircraft in the ocean.

Time stopped as Rattler's heart sank again. He knew the risks and often told new Hawkeye pilots that every aircraft commander at some point had to consider the possibility of a flight where they had to hold the aircraft level while the crew bailed out. The pilot's only chance would be to ditch the aircraft and egress from that point. In fact, years prior, Rattler was flying his own Hawkeye in a dire situation and briefed his crew about that very possibility. He ended up getting his plane back on the carrier successfully, but the thought went through his mind. Now Rattler was flying off the wing of a Hawkeye that the pilot was going to have to ditch. Rattler had his own things to think about now and snapped back into action.

"Red Crown, three-zero-one," Rattler radioed.

"Three-zero-one, go ahead," Red Crown replied.

"Red Crown from three-zero-one, here is an update," Rattler replied, knowing that every high-ranking officer in the battle group was listening. "I have seen four successful parachutes. It seems to me that the pilot is having controllability issues and will try to ditch the aircraft and egress. We are currently at eight hundred feet and descending."

"Three-zero-one, Red Crown copies. Aircraft two-zero-four is the tanker aircraft and is currently ten miles away from the position you marked for bailout. Additionally, the helicopter is en route and about five minutes from the bailout position," Red Crown replied.

"Red Crown, three-zero-one copies all. I plan to stick with the downed aircraft and let two-zero-four stay with the bailout crew," Rattler replied as he was interrupted by the radio altimeter warning going off, telling him he was passing five hundred feet.

"Three-zero-one, copy. Switch button one to coordinate with tower and aircraft two-zero-four," Red Crown called.

"Three-zero-one," Rattler replied as he switched to button one, which was tower frequency, and quickly checked in. "Tower, three-zero-one holding hands with six-zero-one, twenty-five miles south of your position, checking in as SAR on-scene commander, standby," Rattler called.

At that moment, the Hawkeye pilot looked over at Rattler and nodded. He had been switching radios to listen the whole time, and while he was not responding, he was keeping his situational awareness high. He now recognized that Rattler was going to circle overhead after the ditch and help the helicopter come pick him up. It had to make the Hawkeye pilot feel slightly better knowing that someone would know where he was. Rattler was in awe of the calmness that the pilot exuded in his flying and slight mannerisms. While Rattler had thought about what he would do in the same situation, he wasn't sure he would be so calm knowing what was about to happen. Passing three hundred feet, the Hawkeye pilot looked over one last time, gave Rattler a thumbs-up, and then gave the "kiss off" signal, telling Rattler not to follow him any lower.

Rattler leveled at 250 feet over the water and watched helplessly as the Hawkeye continued its descent to its final fate. Time seemed to stop as Rattler watched the Hawkeye crash into the water in what seemed to be slow motion. He banked his aircraft into a tight right-hand turn to keep the aircraft in sight and marked his position. The spray of water from the impact momentarily caused the Hawkeye to disappear, but before Rattler had turned 180 degrees to circle back around, the sea calmed and the Hawkeye sat in the water, the dome sticking out with the fuselage slightly below the water. Rattler immediately passed his position to tower, but it was unnecessary because Rattler caught sight of the rescue helicopter approaching. He kept a tight turn around the downed Hawkeye while listening to the helo pilot approach and pass information on tower frequency.

"Three-zero-one, six-one-two on tower," the helo pilot radioed.

"Go ahead," Rattler replied.

"Six-one-two is taking over as SAR on-scene commander. Aircraft in sight approaching to drop a swimmer," the pilot radioed.

"Copy. Do you need my assistance?" Rattler asked.

"Negative. You are cleared off and back to the ship," the pilot replied.

Rattler was shocked by how matter-of-fact the interaction was, and he was now circling above the wreckage at one thousand feet. He strained his eyes, hoping to see the pilot emerge from the ditching hatch, almost willing the pilot to get out of the plane. He was so focused, but he was shaken out of his situation by the call of "Bingo Bingo," alerting him to his fuel state.

Shit, Rattler thought. He hadn't thought about his fuel since leaving the tanker. He quickly saw where the ship was but wasn't really paying attention to notice if they were still recovering aircraft. His fuel was low, and he needed to get on deck now.

"Tower, three-zero-one checking in 180/15 angels two," Rattler called as he climbed his aircraft slightly to buy some time.

"Three-zero-one copy, case one recover, BRC 330. Charlie," the tower replied, telling Rattler to get on board now.

It was clear weather, daytime, case one, so at least the weather would still be nice. Rattler pushed the power up and dialed in the base recovery course (BRC), which was the direction the carrier was moving, so he could set up his approach. There was no reason for him to do a straight in, and he still needed a day trap to be able to fly that night. The radio was very quiet given everything that was going on, but just like he was taught, there was nothing he could do about the Hawkeye now, and he needed to get his plane on deck.

The carrier came into view just where he thought it would be. He lowered the Bingo warning bug so it wouldn't bother him, and he accelerated and descended to eight hundred feet. He kept a good lookout for other aircraft, but he didn't think anyone else was flying around the ship. As he passed overhead, he could see that the deck was ready; they were not launching any more aircraft. At one mile ahead of the ship, Rattler pulled the power to idle and rolled into a ninety-degree angle of the bank to the left and set up for his landing pattern. His body and brain were working almost subconsciously. He was operating on another level as he configured his gear, flaps, and tailhook for landing and started his approach turn. As he crossed the wake of the aircraft carrier, he saw green "cut lights" from the LSO, clearing him to land. Rattler flew his Hornet with precision and was brought to a stop quickly as his tailhook caught the two wire. For the first time since launch, he exhaled. The adrenaline dumped, and as he held the brakes, his knees started to shake.

CHAPTER NINETEEN

Rattler sat in his room alone, trying to process everything that had just happened. He had landed and debriefed the SDO and intelligence officers and got out of his flight gear. He needed a break, so he went down to his room to take a minute. He sat there alone, looking at a photo of Sandy, when the door opened. He looked up to see Maestro. He could tell he was bringing bad news.

"It was Muncie in six-zero-one, bro. He didn't make it," Maestro said.

Rattler was speechless and frozen. Muncie was a pilot Rattler knew from flight school. Whether he died on impact or he drowned didn't really matter to Rattler; he couldn't get over that he had been the last person to see Muncie alive. He had been super calm and cool and professional and let the rest of his crew survive. Muncie had a wife and two young kids at home who would likely get the news soon, if they hadn't already.

"The rest of the flight schedule has been canceled except for pilots needing CQ. CAG said that anyone needing a night trap could elect not to fly tonight, and they would figure it out. Then the skipper just told the ready room to expect to fly," Maestro continued. "What are you going to do?"

"I guess I'm going to go fly," Rattler replied quietly, trying to process that not only did he just lose a friend, but he also watched him die. That was the thing about aviation that distinguished it from the jobs guys do on the ground. On the ground, they faced death every day in combat, and it was personal; but while Rattler had lost people in the past, most of the time, they took off and just didn't come back. Other than his Hawkeye skipper, until Jackie's failed ejection while they were at training, he had never seen someone die. Even then, the explosion of Jackie's jet somehow prevented Rattler from processing that she had died. Muncie was different. Rattler had been connected to him, flying off his wing until seconds before he died, and Rattler watched it happen on a clear day a few hundred feet away from him. It was forever etched into his mind.

"Dude, I don't think that's a good idea," Maestro said. "Just take CAG up on his offer and take the night off. No one will care."

"I'll think about it, but I don't want to bring attention to myself or have to answer to Skipper," Rattler replied.

"All right. I have to get back to the ready room. Let me know if you need anything," Maestro said as he walked out.

Rattler sat alone in his room once again. While he liked living with just one other person, there were certain times when having a lot of roommates would help. Being alone on an aircraft carrier didn't make things easier. He tried to remember as much as he could about Muncie and their times together in flight school. While not the closest of friends, their paths had crossed a lot, and they spent some time together.

Additionally, Rattler remembered other friends he had lost in the past. He remembered hearing older pilots say that when someone died, it dug up the memories of all the people they lost in the past. It was a trait of aviation that seemed to be constant across all platforms and services. Rattler was living it firsthand now in his stateroom, sitting alone at his steel desk. His sweaty flight suit was unzipped and tied off at the waist. He sipped from a bottle of water and tried to clear his head. On his desk sat a picture of Sandy from their time together on a hiking trip. He loved the photo because it showed both sides of her beauty. When she dressed up to go out, she was drop-dead gorgeous, but in hiking gear, sitting on a rock, worn out from a climb, she exuded just as much beauty to Rattler.

Her smile was radiant, and he tried to harness the positive energy from it to lift his spirits. He looked down at his watch and saw that he had some time before he had to get ready for his night flight. He didn't have anything important to do, so he just stayed in the moment. The truth was Rattler had a ton to do—a Navy pilot was never bored at sea—but nothing seemed to matter right now. Between the flight prior to port, the port call with Sandy, and now Muncie dying, his energy was sapped, and he needed time to recover. Maestro was right. He probably shouldn't fly tonight. But Rattler felt a strong pressure to go fly. He needed some rest, so he got up and went over to his bunk. Completely exhausted, he fell in and was fast asleep after setting his alarm to wake him for his next flight.

CHAPTER TWENTY

The alarm woke Rattler with a start, and he tried to shake off the sleep while he got up and zipped up his flight suit. Looking at his watch, he saw that it was time to go fly, and he needed to get his head in the game. He remembered from his early days of learning to fly in the Navy that compartmentalization was important in this job. Back then, he couldn't imagine what his instructors really meant, but tonight, on an aircraft carrier in the middle of the ocean getting ready to fly, it was obvious.

As he left his room, the mood on the ship seemed different. People were somber as they moved around, and Rattler tried to decide if it was because of the crash or if he was just making it up in his head. As he entered the ready room, he took a deep breath and tried to shake off the day.

The room was quiet as people went about their work and tried to process the death of a member of the air wing. Rattler saw an open computer and checked his watch one more time. He wanted to make sure he had time to check his email before heading up to the jet. As he waited for the unbelievably slow internet connection to link him to the real world, he almost had to laugh. You'd think the greatest warship in the free world would have better internet. He guessed that, for the most part, since everyone and everything he needed to do his job was within the confines of the ship, there really wasn't a need to be connected, and sometimes that was better.

His email popped up, but then he saw there was no connection. His inbox contained a dozen emails that had been delivered, but then it dawned on Rattler that with the mishap and death of a crew member, the ship likely cut the internet connection to prevent information from getting out. This was common practice, and while he couldn't send any emails, he was able to check the messages he had received.

A few emails from work and then one from his parents and one from Sandy brightened his day. It sounded like his mom and dad were doing well, and although they missed him, they were proud of him for the work he was doing. Rattler opened Sandy's email and read each word carefully. She spoke of recent trips she had flown and the cities she had layovers in. She then went on to recount their time together in port and how much fun she had. She half daydreamed of a day when their lives would allow them to live together and spend more time together, but for the time being, she was very proud of Rattler, and her pride showed. She had attached a photo of her layover in Hawaii, but due to the lack of internet connection, Rattler couldn't open it.

He sighed as he closed the email and moved his cursor to the last one in the inbox. He didn't recognize the sender, and there was no subject line. He was immediately transported back to his days on the USS *Nimitz*, flying with the Wallbangers of VAW-117. While he didn't know it at the time, he was right in the middle of a massive treasonous plot to benefit members of his command that would ultimately put Rattler's life in danger. It all started one night when he opened a similar email. Rattler was tempted to just delete this one, but his curiosity got the better of him and he clicked on the email.

"If anyone ever comes up to you and asks you if you want to go fly something, but they can't tell you where you are going or when you'll be back . . . say yes."

—C

He read the email three times and tried to determine who the sender was, but no one came to mind.

"Hey, man. You ready to walk?" Maestro's voice from across the room snapped Rattler out of his daze.

"Oh, crap. Yeah," Rattler replied, glancing at his watch and closing the email. As he went about closing his email inbox and logging off the computer, he noticed the email was no longer in his inbox. He got up and walked to the SDO desk to grab his bag for the flight.

"Sorry, man," Rattler said to Maestro, who was already in his flight gear and ready to walk up to the flight deck. "I'll see you up there. Standard tactical frequency?"

"You got it!" Maestro replied.

The two were going up to get night current again and decided to use a discrete tactical frequency so they could chat during the boring flight. Rattler walked quickly to the maintenance control desk, signed for the aircraft, and then put his flight gear on. His mind swam with thoughts of the email and what happened earlier in the day. Rattler immediately started to think about who could have sent the email, and what they meant by it. When he was ready to fly, he walked out of the gear room and almost ran right into Toad, who was standing by the door.

"Sorry, sir," Rattler said.

"Are you okay, son?" Toad asked.

"Sir?" Rattler asked.

"Listen, I haven't had a chance to talk to you about this, but I know what you saw this afternoon can't be easy on you. Not only did we lose a teammate of this air wing, but you used to fly that plane, and you watched it happen. I'm sure your mind is racing, and if your head isn't in the game, you know you can just cancel the flight. No one would fault you for that if that's what you need to do," Toad exclaimed.

Rattler paused for a moment before replying. His mind was racing. He was still trying to process the day, the death, and the weird email. He was sure Toad was trying to be nice, but he found himself asking himself if he trusted this guy. He wasn't sure, and he didn't have much time to get to his jet and get it ready before launch.

"Thanks, I'll be fine," Rattler replied with a smile and walked to the flight deck, leaving Toad in the passageway. Alone with his thoughts, Rattler tried to put the day into perspective. Sure, today was supposed to be an easy day, but there really wasn't such a thing when you were on an aircraft carrier at sea. When he woke up that morning, all he wanted to do was a little work and two quick flights to get night current around the ship. He knew the importance of night currency and didn't like being on the hit list that CAG would see every day. Now, hours later, he was walking to his jet at night after a day flight that was anything but routine and where he was a SAR on-scene commander and watched a fellow air wing pilot die. He tried to shake it off and get his head in the game.

Chapter Twenty-One

"Three-zero-five Hornet ball four-point-six," Rattler radioed.

"Roger, ball," the LSO replied.

The flight was as mundane as Rattler could have wanted. He launched off the ship and checked in with the appropriate controllers, who all had nothing for him to do. He didn't have a lot of extra gas available, so he mostly flew on autopilot to conserve fuel. After about forty-five minutes of being alone in the cockpit with his thoughts and a few minor conversations with Maestro on the tactical frequency, he started setting up his plane to come back aboard the ship. Time was compressed, as it often is for pilots conducting nighttime carrier operations, and before long, Rattler felt the reassuring tug of the hook of his Hornet grabbing the number three wire and bringing him to a stop. Night currency complete.

It had been a long day, and Rattler was exhausted. After getting out of his flight gear and getting his debrief from the LSOs, he swung by the maintenance desk to write up a few minor things on aircraft 305. Sometimes, he felt bad because it added work for the maintainers, but it was the only way to keep the aircraft in top shape for combat operations. Plus, as a division officer, he knew that keeping the young men and women busy in the maintenance department prevented them from getting in trouble. Lastly, he swung by the ready room, which was empty at this hour, and checked his email.

There was a new one from his parents and one from Sandy telling him that she was on a long layover in Dubai again and how it brought back memories of how they met. He let his mind drift to that night on the roof of a high-rise building in the city when they got to know each other. The connection was immediate and strong, but Rattler couldn't help but think about how different his life was now. Between switching from flying the Hawkeye to the Hornet, moving around the country, and not being married anymore but dating Sandy, it was all a blur. A good blur, but a blur nonetheless.

The last thing Rattler did was try to find the cryptic email. He searched through his inbox and all the other folders he had set up to organize his life on the ship and life at home. Lastly, he went to his deleted messages, but there was nothing there. He sat back for a moment and tried to recall the email from memory.

"If anyone ever comes up to you and asks you if you want to go fly something, but they can't tell you where you are going or when you'll be back . . . say yes."

—C

He had no idea what that meant. Why wouldn't he ask questions if approached in that manner? Who was "C"? So many questions were spinning in his head, he never even heard Maestro come into the room.

"Hey, dude. You okay?" Maestro asked.

"Yeah, sorry. Just daydreaming, I guess," Rattler replied.

"Well, it's nighttime, so not sure that counts. How did your landing go? I got a fair two wire," Maestro said.

"It was fine. Nothing special," Rattler replied as Maestro looked up at the "Greenie Board" in the ready room. It had already been updated from the day, and he saw that Rattler got an OK three wire. All the pilots of the squadron tracked their landings and grades on a huge board on the wall of the ready room. The competition helped, and it showed anyone who walked in who were the best and not-so-good pilots in the squadron. Every squadron competed for "Top Hook" among the other squadrons in the air wing. That was naval aviation, and it made Rattler laugh. It was as if the day-to-day grind of life at sea wasn't tough enough, so they needed to add more competition to keep people sharp.

"Typical. OK three wire," Maestro said. "You're making us look bad."

"Just lucky, man," Rattler replied. "I need to get some sleep."

With that, Rattler gave up and closed his email. The mysterious one was gone, leaving more questions than answers. Maybe it had been sent to the wrong person, and the sender redacted it, or maybe his mind was playing tricks on him. At this point, there was no way to know. He just wanted to grab a shower and sleep this day off.

CHAPTER TWENTY-TWO

Sandy walked down the street looking in the shop windows slowly, trying to pass the time. She normally went out with her fellow flight attendants, but she was comfortable in Dubai, and it was the middle of the day. Her friends were sleeping off a late-night party that she didn't want to go to, so she was up early and wanted to get some fresh air. She looked at nothing in particular as she strolled past the stores selling expensive clothing and jewelry. Her mind wandered back to the night she met Rattler. He seemed shy and understated at the party her friend Cheri had made her go to. Sandy was immediately taken aback by his matter-of-fact good looks and charm. He didn't act like he was trying to impress anyone and seemed like a sweet and genuine man. Her instincts were correct, and since that night, every one of her free thoughts was occupied by the American Navy pilot who stole her heart.

The street was busy, and her mind wandered, which is why she probably didn't notice him. Approaching from behind, a man in jeans and a plain T-shirt bumped into her hard and grabbed her purse. Everything happened so fast. One moment, she was walking in the warm sun, and the next, she was on the ground, watching the man disappear into the crowd with her purse. As she tried to regain her composure, she felt a pain in her side, and when she reached down, she felt something warm through her shirt. Pulling her hand back, she saw it was covered in blood. Her head immediately felt heavy, and her eyes struggled to stay open. She laid her head back, hearing screams, and thought about Rattler's smile one last time.

"Shit!" Rattler said out loud as he sprang straight up, hitting his head on the top of the bunk bed in his room. Closing his eyes again and then opening them to try to refocus, he took in his surroundings. He was in his room, on the ship . . . It was a dream. More of a nightmare, really. His heart rate beat through the roof, and he could feel his blood pumping in the vein in his neck, similar to how it did when he was preparing to land on the ship. His hands were shaking, and he was soaked in sweat.

"Dude, you okay?" Maestro asked from the other bunk. He had been awakened by Rattler.

"Yeah, shit. Sorry, man. Bad dream," Rattler replied.

"Okay, dude. Sorry about that. I'm waving today, so I'm going to try to get some more sleep. Let me know if you need anything, okay?" Maestro replied.

"Yeah, man. Again, sorry I woke you." Rattler got out of bed and tried to shake the dream.

He walked around to the other side of the room and turned the light on above the sink. He wanted to keep the room as dark as possible so Maestro could get back to sleep. He saw the flight schedule had been slid under the door, so he went to take a look. Night combat flight as a wingman was what he was scheduled for. Almost immediately after reading the schedule, Rattler heard the phone ring. He grabbed it quickly so that Maestro could get some sleep.

"Hello?" Rattler answered.

"Dude, sorry if I woke you, but I need you in the ready room ASAP. You've been moved up to the day launch because of a sick out.

You're going in-country and need to brief as soon as you can get up here," the SDO replied.

"On my way," Rattler answered as he hung up the phone.

He immediately went into go mode. He had plans to work out, go talk to his shops, make sure his enlisted guys and girls were doing okay on deployment, and then get ready for his flight. Now he was behind, and if he hated anything on the ship, it was being behind. Rushing caused mistakes, and mistakes could be fatal on an aircraft carrier. Rattler threw his flight suit on and checked his pocket for the cross from his aunt. It was exactly where it was supposed to be. No need to start the day off with some bad karma.

As he laced up his boots, his mind wandered back to the dream he had. It seemed so vivid and real, but he knew that he was over-tired and probably wasn't sleeping well on the ship anyway. Add to that the food and noise, and his dreams always seemed more real on the ship. He tried to put it out of his mind because he had work to do. After checking that he had everything he needed, he sanitized his flight suit by pulling off all the patches and his rank, so that, if he ever found himself behind enemy lines, he would have nothing to identify who he was. He always flew this way when on combat missions, but he found it funny. It would be obvious who he was if he ever had to get out of the aircraft, and he could always rip the patches off on the ground. At any rate, it was SOP, so he did it. He didn't like flying without his name tag though, because that is where his wings of gold were stitched, and he didn't like flying without his wings. He knew it was a stupid superstition, but it still bugged him.

Rattler half jogged to the ready room and got there just as Toad came back in the other door. It looked like he would be the flight lead and Rattler would be the wingman. Rattler grabbed the briefing cards from Toad and sat down to listen to him give the details of the flight. They were fairly simple overall. They would launch and hit a Super Hornet tanker overhead the ship to make sure they could take gas and then head north into bad guy country. They would hit a tanker, which looked like a KC-10 tanker, on the way in. That made Rattler happy because he liked the KC-10. It had the ability to use a boom or long hose for tanking.

They typically used the hose for Navy jets because the pilots were used to it. The KC-135, on the other hand, was affectionately called the Iron Maiden because it only had a boom with a short hose. It gave pilots like Rattler a lot less slop to handle the tanking. When he was tired and trying to get gas, he wanted it to be as easy as possible.

He scanned the tanker list. It looked like the first time he would hit the Iron Maiden for gas was on the way out of country and heading back home. That was not ideal since he would be at his most fatigued at that point, but on the plus side, he would be flying during the day, so that would help for sure. Additionally, they would be working with a SEAL team on the ground who would track a high-value target and provide overwatch. Not the most exciting mission he could ask for, but also not the worst. The high-value targets tended to be jumpy, and things often heated up very quickly. Maybe he would see some action and help the SEALs on the ground as well. Then they would head back to the ship tank once off the KC-135 and then hit the Super Hornet before a day landing. *Just another day at sea*, Rattler thought as he listened to Toad and played the flight through his head.

"So, our biggest issue is that the kill box that we are working has tall mountains to the east. Keep that in mind with regard to the terrain, but also keep your eyes peeled, because the intel brief said that SAMs were being placed at higher altitudes to be able to reach out and touch us more. While the likelihood is slim, it is still a treat. At least it's daytime, right?" Toad joked. "Okay, take a minute to eat something and hit the head, and I'll see you on the flight deck. You feeling up for this?"

"Yup, let's do it," Rattler replied.

In reality, he really wasn't feeling up for it, but there was nothing specifically wrong either. Maybe it was time for a break, as something was nagging at him, but he couldn't put his finger on it. He chalked it up to being a little burnt out on deployment, which he had experienced before when he was a Hawkeye pilot. He figured at this point in his career he would have been used to it, but maybe everyone got burnt out at some point. At least it was a day flight. Those were few and far between during combat ops, but he would take it when he got the opportunity.

Rattler walked to the forward wardroom quickly and grabbed a peanut butter sandwich, which he ate in three bites as he made a second for the flight. He also grabbed an apple and two energy bars before heading to the jet. The flight was scheduled for six hours, and he knew he would be hungry before he got back. It didn't seem like much; but, for the most part, he would be just sitting on his ass in the jet on autopilot except for the launch, recovery, and tanking portions. Not really expending a ton of energy unless something got interesting with the SEALs, which was unlikely.

He quickly hit the head and put on his flight gear, then swung by the maintenance control desk to see that he would be flight aircraft 311, his jet. Unlike the movies, where pilots always seemed to fly aircraft with their names on them, the real world was the luck of the draw. He did like flying 311 because he felt connected to the aircraft, but that was likely just a weird thing he made up in his own mind. Each jet was essentially the same, and while some had their own little idiosyncrasies, they all got the job done. Rattler signed for the jet and made his way topside to the flight deck.

CHAPTER TWENTY-THREE

It was a beautiful clear day, and the flight deck was humming as the flight deck crews prepared to launch aircraft and quickly recover those airborne. A typical day of cyclic operations around the ship. Every hour or so, a new group of aircraft would launch and then the airborne would recover. Repeat that ten to twelve times a day, every day at sea . . . that was a deployment. It was easy to get complacent, but being in the world's most dangerous environment—the flight deck of an aircraft carrier—helped keep people sharp. Rattler watched the whole scene while walking to his aircraft and trying to enjoy the moment. This is what he worked so hard for. In college, flight school, and even his time with the Hawkeye squadron—everything he did was to one day have the opportunity to fly fighter aircraft off an aircraft carrier into combat. The road he took may not have been the most traveled, but it got him here, and he was happy with how it turned out.

He approached aircraft 311 and returned the salute of his plane captain, who had the jet ready to go. After checking that the correct number of preflight pins had been removed, he began his walk around, and after he was confident the jet was good to go, he climbed the ladder and strapped in. He immediately felt one with the machine. With each buckle, he strapped himself into the machine, but it became more of an extension of his body. A lethal extension at that. His hands were flipping switches, and his eyes were looking at screens without a conscience thought. He had done it hundreds of times before, and the sequence became routine, but if the littlest thing was out of place, he would notice it immediately.

Today seemed like a perfect day. The air boss called out to start the jets over the 5MC. Rattler fired up the engines and quickly closed the canopy to try to get his aircraft to the catapult first. He wanted to be off the deck quickly and hit the tanker overhead so that Toad wasn't waiting on him. Doing his best to be a good wingman started with always being ahead. He succeeded, and very quickly the yellow shirt was taxiing him to catapult 3 on the waist. He would be the first to launch off the waist catapults, and he could already see the Super Hornet tanker overhead.

While waiting for the launch to begin and sitting on the catapult, Rattler took a moment to ensure everything was set. Being ahead and fast was good, but as a single-seat pilot, there was no one else to catch his mistakes. He ran his fingers over all the switches one more time to ensure everything was set and checked his pocket for his dog tags and cross, which were exactly where they should be. Before long, the flight deck crew was showing him a weight board. He gave a thumbs-up in return, and the process was in motion.

A small taxi forward to get the aircraft launch bar into the shuttle on the catapult, and it seemed like only moments passed before Rattler saw the "run it up" signal from the shooter. Rattler advanced the throttles to military power, scanned his instruments, and did a full wipe out of the controls before looking back to see the shooter giving the "raise the roof" signal for Rattler to select full afterburner. Once he did that, he saluted with his right hand, held on to the towel rack handle on the canopy, and kept his left hand full forward on the throttles. Final checks were done outside, and soon Rattler and aircraft 311 were rocketing down the catapult and were airborne. In full go mode, Rattler raised the gear and flew the departure outside of five miles before climbing and joining on the tanker overhead. All of his systems were working perfectly, and he smiled as he thought about how happy he was with "his" jet being so good.

Once overhead, he topped off his gas from the Super Hornet mission tanker and waited for Toad to get his fuel. Once both were satisfied their aircraft were good to go and they had enough gas for the first part of the flight, they departed the overhead stack and headed north toward bad guy country. Rattler felt remarkably calm for this flight. Things had seemed to settle down for him, and he was caught back up with the mission for the day. He flew his aircraft approximately one mile abeam Toad's jet and made sure he had the cockpit organized. Kneeboard cards from the mission briefing were the main thing to keep in order, as they had all the information with regard to call signs, tanker frequencies, and what they were expected to do. Once all of that was taken care of, he took a deep breath and took in the views below. Desert, mostly all desert, as they went "feet dry" and ran their checklists.

All of this was done without so much as a word between Toad and Rattler. Rattler found that odd. He knew Toad as a pretty quiet guy, and even more so when he was flying. Regardless, Rattler remained calm and tried to focus his mind on the task ahead. The hardest part at this point was not getting complacent. He had seen it before, and he almost felt the vibe that the squadron and ship were getting complacent on this deployment. There wasn't much going on, and while some crews were dropping bombs or shooting the gun, a lot more were coming back to the ship with all their weapons, and it was starting to take its toll on the pilots. No one wanted to be here without doing the job they trained for. For Rattler, it was a little bit tougher, because when he was on deployments in the E-2C, he would watch aircraft come back day and night "completely Winchester," or out of weapons from their mission. Rattler wanted that feeling of accomplishment and was still looking for it.

Before long, Rattler and Toad found themselves joining on a KC-10 tanker to get more gas. Such was the life of an F/A-18C pilot—always paying attention to their fuel, and it seemed like always looking for more gas. After tanking this time, they were halfway to their position, which they would hold to support the SEALs for a few hours. Rattler had been in-country before, but this was his first time during the day. Most operations were at night, and he found himself getting distracted by his surroundings. At times, it was hard to see from his vantage point what anyone was fighting for because it seemed like there was a whole lot of nothing out there. After that last tank, Toad and Rattler would soon check in with their controller on the ground and transition to yo-yo tanking, meaning that one of them would always stay on station and the other would go to the tanker. That way, the SEALs never lost their air cover. As the section of Hornets flew farther north and away from the relative safety of the ship, Rattler settled in. It was going to be a long flight.

CHAPTER TWENTY-FOUR

"Rattler, you up?" Toad asked on the tactical frequency.

"Yeah, what's up?" Rattler replied, Toad's voice snapping him back to reality as he had settled into his flight sitting on station, listening to the SEALs on the ground not doing much at all.

"I'm coming off station to get gas early. Figured it's better to have it if we need it. You have the lead," Toad said.

"Copy, I have the lead," Rattler replied.

While Toad coordinated with the SEALs on the ground to switch responsibilities to Rattler, Rattler sat there at twenty-five thousand feet in the air in his Hornet, trying to stay focused. At times like these, his mind tended to race faster than it should. Using the Hornet's sensors, he could tell that Toad didn't need fuel yet, so he found it odd he was leaving early. At any rate, he checked off station, leaving Rattler alone and the only set of eyes watching over the SEAL team on the ground. All was quiet and likely would stay that way. Nothing happened during the day. Rattler couldn't remember the last time he saw a plane come back from a day mission after expending its ordnance. It seemed like the enemy would go to sleep during the day and wreak havoc at night.

Rattler let out a deep sigh and continued to scan his surroundings to stay alert. His inside/outside scan included checking his ATFLIR to ensure nothing was happening on the ground while looking outside to scan the sky and mountains around him. His Hornet had been on autopilot since they checked on station, and he was fighting the mundane life of a combat pilot, waiting for something to happen. After a few minutes, he reached into his helmet bag on the right side of the cockpit and pulled out an apple. *The small luxuries of flying a fighter aircraft*, he thought, and he took a bite. His mask dangled on the left side of his helmet as it had for a while now. It was a rule to wear it from takeoff to landing, but few pilots did. It was uncomfortable, got in the way, and was more of a nuisance during downtimes flying.

Communications between aircraft were usually minimal, and even more so today flying with Toad, so there was really no need to keep it on. Of course, like everything in aviation, there were risks involved in not wearing it. If he lost cabin pressurization, he would have only a few seconds to get it back on before he went hypoxic from the lack of oxygen at this altitude, but that was a risk Rattler, like most pilots, took to be more comfortable on long flights.

As the plane banked to the left to stay on its prescribed orbit, which would allow Rattler to keep his ATFLIR on the target, he finished his apple and put the core back in his helmet bag. After stowing the bag again to his right, he put his head back against the seat and closed his eyes for a second. At times like these, he wondered if transitioning to the Hornet was worth it. He had been at the top of his game in the Hawkeye, and while it was challenging and fun to switch to flying the Hornet, he was not sure if he had made the right decision. When flying the Hawkeye, he dreamt about the exciting and adrenaline-inducing flights in the Hornet, and during training, there was a lot of that. Today, however, like a lot of combat flights, he sat trying to keep his mind sharp while waiting for something to happen that likely wouldn't before it was their time to head back to the ship.

He decided that he wasn't going to find the answer today and let his mind drift to thoughts of Sandy. The mental picture of her in the hot tub in Dubai or wearing only his T-shirt back at his house in Lemoore brought a smile across his face. She was quite a sight to behold, and he felt very lucky that Clipper had met her and brought her and Cherri to the party in Dubai. How his life had changed since then.

"Rage one-two, you up?" radioed the SEAL on the ground.

"Go," Rattler replied.

"Hey, brother. I'm going to take a piss. I'll be comm out for five mikes. I'll check back in when I get back," the SEAL answered.

"Rage one-two," Rattler replied.

Breaking his daydreaming, Rattler went back to checking his sensors and aircraft systems to see if everything was still working okay. Then he checked on Toad. He was almost at the tanker, but two other aircraft were there as well, so it looked like Rattler would be alone for a little while. That suited him just fine. He had spent a lot of his flying time sharing the plane with others, and he welcomed the quiet. Settling back into his daydream after he was satisfied that everything was still okay, he brought his mind back to Sandy. Her smile, her eyes, her voice . . . They were so peaceful and warm . . .

BEEP, BEEP, BEEP. The sound squawked into Rattler's headset, shaking him from his peaceful reverie as he tried to figure out what the noise was. His world immediately changed when he realized it was his radar warning receiver (RWR) gear warning of a launched missile that was aimed at him. He immediately grabbed the stick and throttles and disengaged the autopilot while scanning outside of the cockpit to try to pick up the missile visually. A glance to his left and then his right indicated nothing until he looked further right, just in time to see the missile approach from his right rear quadrant, slightly low. Time slowed and then stopped as Rattler slammed out chaff and flares in a last-ditch effort to confuse the missile, but as he rolled the plane to the right and cut the power, he realized it was too late. He felt the impact before he heard anything, as his

Hornet, which was perfect just seconds prior, now lurched forward and groaned as if it were in pain. Rattler's hands were working the stick and throttles in an effort to control the aircraft, but even before his brain could process that his control inputs were not having any effect, he was met with more noise. The plane started to protest.

"Engine fire left. Engine fire right," the aircraft announced repeatedly as Rattler looked forward at the display panel, only to be met by more red warning and amber caution lights than he had ever seen before. With every passing second, more seemed to illuminate, and with them, time slowed further. Rattler's brain tried to process what was happening, but all signs were clear to him. The missile had impacted, and he had no choice other than to eject. He glanced up at the mirrors on the canopy bow to check the aircraft's tail section and wished he hadn't. At that moment, he realized there was nothing left of the aircraft. His hands left the stick and throttle and moved swiftly to the ejection handle between his legs. As he pulled with all his might, his final thought was, *God, please let my parents know that I love them.*

CHAPTER TWENTY-FIVE

"General quarters, general quarters. All hands man your battle stations. Forward and up to starboard, down, and aft to port. Set material condition 'Zebra' throughout the ship. This is NOT a drill," sounded over the 1MC in the ready room as Maestro sat at the SDO desk, trying to look through emails.

"Shit, there goes any chance of emailing home," he said to no one in particular.

The phone rang immediately, and as Maestro answered, the words he heard stopped him in his tracks. "Three-one-one is down. Start the mishap protocol." Without a word, Maestro turned to the giant whiteboard behind him to confirm what he already knew. His roommate was down. Without knowing any more details and almost immediately, the ready room burst into activity as the word spread around the ship instantly. The skipper, the XO, and most of the pilots sprang into action, running the mishap checklist as they tried to gather what little information they could.

Rattler was flying in aircraft 311, and Toad was on the tanker when the missile impacted the Hornet. Toad was immediately recalled to the ship and was en route now, but he would not be able to provide much more information than they already had. As members of the Warhawks frantically tried to accomplish everything on the checklist in the required time, Maestro sat in shock, trying to make sense of it all. Just this morning he and Rattler had been in the room chatting it up, and now for all he knew, his roommate was down behind enemy lines trying to survive. It all happened so fast that Maestro couldn't process it. The phone kept ringing, and everyone was asking questions, but there were no answers. No one could even remember the last time a plane was shot at, let alone shot down during this seemingly never-ending conflict. The pilots had all gone through the motions of filling out their blood chits and carrying their sidearms, but no one really expected to need it. Now the best-case scenario was that Rattler was on the ground in hostile territory trying to evade capture, but that was assuming he made it out of the aircraft.

After losing their air wing mate in the Hawkeye and now this, the atmosphere of the ship immediately took on a different vibe. It was like war had knocked on their front door, and those who never really had to deal with it and felt relatively safe aboard the ship were thrust into the real consequences of the dangers of deployment. Maestro answered the phone to hear that Toad had successfully landed and was heading to intel to debrief CAG and the skipper. Flight operations were suspended until further notice, and no emails were to leave the ship, not that they could.

The first thing that happens during a general quarters is the ship cuts the internet connection for most of the people onboard. Only a select few had accounts that could break through the firewall, and Maestro didn't know anyone with that access. The whole idea was information control. Since there were more questions than answers, the Navy knew it was better to keep the outside world in the dark, for the most part, rather than let the rumor train get going. Families at home would worry, and it would spread like wildfire. Better to shut that down until there were answers. It was the only way to control it, but it didn't make it easier for either side. Maestro sat for a moment and said a silent prayer for his friend; then he got to work. It was the only thing he could do to help.

Chapter Twenty-Six

Everything hurt. Rattler tried to move, but every part of his body was in pain—searing pain. He couldn't see, but his other senses felt like they were on overload. His brain was scrambled, and he tried to control his breathing. Lying still seemed to be the only thing that calmed him, so he did that. He focused on one small thing at a time. He knew his head was still attached based on the headache he had. He slowly inhaled through his nose, which seemed to help. Then he swallowed. His mouth was incredibly dry, but he could still swallow. He tried to move each finger just a little, but his mind kept losing track. He hoped they were all there. He continued to take personal inventory of his injuries moving down his body. He felt pain in his left knee, an old football injury, and his ankle. Trying the best he could, he moved each toe, and although his brain couldn't count to ten, he hoped they were all there, or at least most of them.

Although he still couldn't see anything, his brain started to awaken. It was like he had been in the deepest sleep of his life. He almost couldn't tell if he was even awake, but he must be, as his brain was starting to process things. There was light behind his eyes, but his brain would not allow them to open. It was almost as if his brain was locked onto trying to figure something else out, but he couldn't process what it was. He remembered in survival training that they spoke about taking personal inventory first. Once that was done, you should inventory your surroundings and your gear and get back into the fight. If you did it out of order, you may not notice an injury or move before realizing the enemy was nearby. *Slow is fast*, he thought as he started at the top again. The headache was still there, check. Deeper breath this time. Still breathing; that was good. As he tried to swallow, it was like his brain immediately snapped awake. That smell: something wasn't right. It smelled too clean, too medical, antiseptic-like in nature, and nothing like that would be near the crash site of an aircraft. Then, as his brain continued to broaden its understanding of where he was, something else became clear. He was cold, surprisingly cold for being in the desert. It didn't make sense. It was like Rattler's mind was trying to process what it could step by step and would add an additional sense once he comprehended the previous one. First was the smell, then the cold, and then the light. The pain in his eyes subsided enough for him to realize that the light behind his eyelids wasn't natural. At that moment, he heard it—the low hum of fluorescent lights. His eyes opened slowly to process where he was. It was a light gray medical room of some sort that he couldn't place. It didn't look like any hospital he had ever seen. There were no windows and only one door at the far end of the room. He was in a bed and was hooked to medical machines. An IV was in his left arm, and when he saw it, his body was almost overcome with pain. Everything hurt from head to toe, and he almost threw up. He took deep breaths, trying to control himself and not lose what little he had eaten seemingly forever ago.

After settling down, he opened his eyes again and looked himself over. The good news was that he had all his limbs. His flight suit was gone, and he was dressed in some sort of medical gown, but it didn't look like anything he had seen before. The room and the gown made him realize this wasn't a hospital at all. It definitely had a clinical feel, but he still didn't know where he was.

As he continued his physical inventory, he heard footsteps. Nothing too loud. He tried to count them. It sounded like just a single person. He could hear no words. There was a single door and no other way to escape. His brain had transitioned to the survival portion of his training. Until he knew where he was, he had to assume he was on his own, and he needed to find a way out, back to his ship and squadron. They had to know he was down and would have heard the emergency locator transmitter (ELT) from the ejection seat. He was sure that people would be looking for him.

As he tried to calm his breathing and come up with a plan, the door opened slowly. A tall, thin man slowly looked in as if to see if Rattler was awake. As he walked into the room, Rattler decided he would look the man over and not speak first. *Take inventory of your surroundings and give them nothing that could be used against you later on.* He was surprised his training was kicking in. It had been years since he was in the mountains of Maine in the snow, learning how to evade and also be a prisoner of war. That thought hit him hard. That's what he was now. A prisoner.

As the tall man approached the bedside, Rattler didn't say a word but tried to assess the situation. The man was about Rattler's height, he'd guess six foot three or six foot four inches tall. He was a slender man, but one who saw physical activity on a daily basis. He wore dark gray military pants of some sort that didn't look like they had ever seen dirt. Everything from his combat boots to his shirt exuded a sense of being properly worn and in the correct place. The man gave the impression that if he had scuffed his shoe, he would throw it away and buy a new pair. He wore a tactical black watch on his left wrist. Not a cheap one either. Rattler couldn't place the exact model, but he recognized that it was a Breitling automatic. The webbed band and dark case made it look like it was ready for anything. He didn't see many combatants wearing such a watch, mainly because of the price, but also because Breitling was known for being an aviator's watch. This briefly puzzled Rattler, but as his training taught him, he was trying to notice the little details. *Focus on the little things and the bigger picture will come into view.*

The man stood briefly as if he was conducting the same analysis on Rattler. The two could not have been more opposite, as Rattler looked like he just lost a bout against a prized fighter, and this man looked like he just stepped out of a tactical gear catalog. There was something different about him, though. Rattler noticed it immediately. While everything on the man was perfectly in place, he didn't look like an impostor. He looked like a man who had seen things and done things that most do not. He looked like a man on a mission, a man who was used to being in control and having things work out in his favor. While he looked like the sort of man who calculated everything over and over in his head, he also looked like a man who would stop at nothing to accomplish the goal. Rattler could see this in the man's eyes. After Rattler's gaze moved from the man's boots to his pants to his watch, he rested on the man's eyes. You can learn a lot about someone from their eyes. Rattler wasn't sure where he had learned this, but he seemed to always know it. Maybe it was something he picked up from his father when he was young. He remembered his father teaching him how to shake hands. He said to always stand up and look someone in the eyes when you shake their hand. Rattler wasn't in a hand-shaking mood, but this man's eyes caught him. They were strong, and his gaze never wavered. As he assessed Rattler in the same way Rattler was assessing him, his eyes were laser focused—like the window to a giant supercomputer that was taking in as much data as quickly as possible to formulate a solution to a problem.

Rattler lay in the bed as the moments hung in the air. Seconds ticked by as both men locked in, trying to assess the other. Rattler didn't feel threatened, but he also didn't feel comfortable. He was fairly sure this man wasn't here to kill him, but he was also unsure if he was there to help. The man moved closer in a calculated way that made Rattler nervous. He glanced around the room to remind himself that there was only one way out, and it was through his visitor. Not that it was an option, because Rattler was stuck in bed with IVs attached to him and in so much pain that even blinking his eyes hurt. Rattler realized he was all but helpless and decided that if this was it, he would never take his eyes off the man. Locked onto the man's dark blue eyes, Rattler was so focused on each second that it was exhausting. It felt like only moments ago he had been flying his Hornet high above the earth, and now he was here. His brain couldn't understand the time difference or how long it had been. While he tried to calculate it and piece it all together, the man took one more step to the side of the bed and finally spoke.

"Son, I know you are confused, and there will be time to fill you in on everything, but that time is not now." The man spoke in an unassuming voice that matched the rest of his persona. Then it hit Rattler: the thing that was truly remarkable about this stranger was that nothing was remarkable. He stood out because nothing stood out. He was the type of person you would bump into on the street and never remember a single detail about him. It was incredible how everything about him seemed to be specifically designed to not grab your attention.

"I can assure you that you are safe; your medical condition is stable, and you are at no risk of long-term effects from your ejection," the man continued. "I have to ask you one question, and I need an immediate answer. Your answer will dictate how we proceed going forward. I need you to come fly for me. I cannot tell you what you will be flying or when you will get back. The mission and details will present themselves in due time, but for the time being, I need a simple yes or no."

Chapter Twenty-Seven

The old man had received an encrypted message while out on his property and immediately made his way back to the main house of his estate. This was the news he was looking forward to getting, and he found himself almost giddy with anticipation. As he drove up the main driveway, he looked over his property. Everything in front of him was his. He thought back on his family lineage and contemplated how, over a few generations, his family went from dirt-floor poor to one of the richest families in the country. It was nice, but he cared very little about any of it. He could trade it all tomorrow if he had to. His wife was gone, and the children were more than taken care of and would want for nothing for the rest of their lives. He could buy anything that interested him immediately, and it wouldn't make the slightest dent in his portfolio. None of that mattered to him. What got him up in the morning and kept him going through the day was the power. His control over others to make them do what he wanted, the fear of the men below him, and the ability to dictate their futures with one phone call are what separated him from his father. His father made huge gains in their family's financial future, which undoubtedly helped his own venture, but he did it the clean way. His father wasn't interested in power, only wealth. That is where they differed. When you have everything, the only thing left you could possibly want is power . . . At least that's what the old man thought as he walked up the steps to his estate and made his way to his office to check his email.

He said nothing to any of the people he came across and immediately sat at his desk and logged into his computer, past the various firewalls that protected his information. Every second seemed like a lifetime, and he couldn't wait to confirm the news he was hoping for. After finally getting past all the protections, he opened his secret email and saw what he was looking for. He double-clicked the email, and it opened in a separate window. It simply read: "It is done."

The old man read it three or four times to confirm what it said and then reclined in his overstuffed office chair. Looking past his desk to the window and the view of his estate, a smile crept across his face. In his mind, the ultimate power was dictating and controlling others. He had decided that this Navy lieutenant was in his way, and he used his power to eliminate the problem. The ultimate game, he thought, was hunting humans, and that is effectively what he had done. The threat was no longer there, and his mission could continue. Sure, some had died that he could have used, but ultimately, he would adapt and overcome, just as his father had taught him. The plan was working. He still held all the cards and, more importantly, all the power. He closed his email and logged off his computer. Filled with the joy of winning, he finally relaxed.

CHAPTER TWENTY-EIGHT

The ship had been a mess since general quarters was called, and the internet was still down. Toad had returned to the ship and was debriefed by the intelligence officer, skipper, and XO before returning to the ready room. Obviously, everyone had questions, but there really weren't any answers. Toad was on the tanker when Rattler was shot down, and when he returned, all hell had broken loose. The SEALs on the ground had split into two groups—one to stay with the high-value asset they were tracking and the other to make their way to the crash site and try to rescue or recover Rattler. The main problem they faced was the distance and terrain between where they were and where it appeared Rattler's Hornet had crashed. Toad tried to get information from the SEAL team commander, but there was little there too. Rattler had not said anything on the radio frequency; all of a sudden, he was just gone. Toad briefly heard the ELT from Rattler's ejection seat, but shortly after he heard it, the signal was gone. This could have been a malfunction, or it could have been turned off manually. The latter was unlikely because it was that signal that would help friendly forces get to Rattler, but nothing could be ruled out at this point. For all anyone knew, Rattler could have not survived the ejection or had maybe been captured and taken prisoner.

As Maestro sat and listened intently to Toad telling the other members of the squadron what had happened, something didn't add up. He had been on his fair share of combat missions and had done a lot of "yo-yo" tanking, but he and his wingman would always communicate the whole time they were separated. It helped for many reasons, but a significant one is that it kept both pilots engaged in the mission so that when the first got back from the tanker, they were ready to take over immediately while the second left to tank.

Toad kept saying how little communication he and Rattler had over the tactical frequency that whole flight. That seemed odd to Maestro. At some point, he was over the day and left the ready room to head to his stateroom and try to process everything. As he opened the door, the reality of the situation hit him like a fist to the face. The room was empty, but all of Rattler's things were there. A spare flight suit hung in the corner next to his desk, which held photos of Sandy at the beach and the car Rattler was working on. Next to that was a photo of his parents, which made Maestro have to sit down. Somewhere on the ground in Afghanistan, his roommate was either captured or trying to survive, and seeing his parents was too much for Maestro. The internet was still not working, so Maestro sat down at his desk and started writing a letter to Rattler's parents. He didn't know what to say, but he knew his emotions at the moment were strong and whatever came out would likely be something they would want to hear.

CHAPTER TWENTY-NINE

Rattler woke up with a start and almost sat completely upright. His body ached immediately, and he was reminded of his condition. As his eyes adjusted, he realized he wasn't in the same room he had been in previously. He didn't have any perspective of time and didn't know how long he had been asleep. His mouth was dry, and there was a glass of water on the table next to the bed. As he took a sip, he realized his current surroundings were much nicer than the previous room. While this was clearly still a medical room of some sort, it looked like a longer-term stay facility. The furnishings gave a sense of comfort and warmth. The temperature in the room was perfect for sleep—slightly cold, but not too cold.

He went back to his training: personal inventory first. Starting at his head and moving down, he tried to move each part of his body. Other than a headache, he didn't feel any worse than he would after finishing a hard workout. While he was beat-up, his body seemed to be functioning, and he had the ability to move. He also realized that he was not hooked up to any machines anymore. Bandages on his arms from the IVs were all that was left.

Next, it was time to inventory his surroundings. Like in the previous room, there was a door at the far end. There was a single comfortable bed, and in the corner, there was a couch. Directly across from the couch, there was a small metal desk and a chair. The furnishings were sparse but livable, for sure. Additionally, this room had windows—two of them opposite the door—and Rattler could see sunshine from behind the curtains. Although he didn't see any cameras, he had to believe he was being monitored.

Having completed the inventory of his condition and his surroundings, he decided the best thing to do was to lie still for a little bit and listen. You could learn a lot about where you are from the surrounding sounds. At first, he heard nothing—no sounds at all that he could discern—but as his heart rate slowed and his breathing calmed, he began to make out sounds. Not the sounds of people or animals, but industrial sounds. Sounds of heavy machinery started to stand out. He was instantly transported back to his survival training.

He remembered the cold Maine winter morning as if it were yesterday. Sitting in his cell after being captured and having gone through waterboarding and physical abuse, he sat on the floor of his room listening. He heard the cries of others and the constant sound of either music playing or babies crying to get inside the heads of the student prisoners. Then it all stopped, and out of nowhere, the industrial sounds began. In Rattler's mind, it sounded like buses, and he let his mind go where it shouldn't. He envisioned himself being released from his cell and walking to the comfortable bus to go back to base to get a shower and a meal. His mood instantly lifted as he saw the end of the training in sight.

Unfortunately, this was a classic tactic used on prisoners of war, because he was taken out of his cell, along with the rest of his classmates, only to be met with more physical labor and interrogations. He learned that day that mental torture can be far more damning than physical torture.

He blinked his eyes to focus again on the sounds he was hearing. It was definitely different types of heavy machinery. He could tell some were trucks, and he thought he also heard the distinct sound of helicopters starting up. His spirits lifted momentarily as he thought he might be on some Air Force base and safe, but he remembered his training and stayed focused and still. *Control what you can control;* that was what he taught. Under the current circumstances, he felt the best thing to do was wait. Lie still and wait. He had water, and he wasn't particularly hungry, so he lay in bed and tried to control his mind. He thought about Sandy and his parents and how worried they must be. Also, he wondered what the members of the Warhawks were doing right now. If they were still looking for him or if life aboard the ship had gone back to normal. While he had been in the Navy for the better part of a decade, he had never experienced something like this, so it was hard to tell how carrier life would be. His thoughts came back to his parents, and he knew that the Navy wouldn't tell them anything until they knew more. His parents were smart. His mother would worry right away when the emails stopped, but his dad would keep his cool. Inside, he would be tearing himself apart trying to figure out what happened, but he would never show it. Emotions were not something his dad showed outwardly.

As Rattler considered what his friends and family were going through, he heard the steps. Distinct footsteps of heavy boots on a metal floor. It was the first signs of human life since he had woken up. He heard them approach from afar and stop outside of the door. Rattler's mind immediately focused as he looked around the room for some sort of weapon. There was very little to choose from, and what was there was too far to get to quickly. There was the metal chair that was on the other side of the room, but he couldn't get to it, so the calmer part of his brain prevailed, and he just stayed put. Clearly, whoever was holding Rattler could have killed him if they wanted to. He was completely exposed in this room, and the job would have been easy. Rattler assumed he must be useful to them in some way, so he waited. The sound of the knob on the door turning echoed in the room. Ratter's mind raced to imagine who was on the other side. The only thing he knew was he was not on the ship, and he was not at home. It could be anyone about to open the door, and he had to be prepared. He remembered his father telling him to not show his fear, and he decided at that moment that no matter who walked through the door, he would lie still and show no reaction. As the door opened and light flooded the room, Rattler's eyes focused on the figure who stood in the doorway. Absolute shock swept over him. The air was sucked from his lungs, and his mouth hung open, unable to speak.

CHAPTER THIRTY

"Dude, you look like crap!" Clipper said, standing in the doorway with a smile, continuing before Rattler could speak. "Look, man, I'm just happy you're okay. I know you have a ton of questions right now, and I don't blame you for wanting to know all the answers, but you need to stay calm and relax. You still have a lot of recovering to do, and I don't want to get that blood pressure too high too fast. There will be time for that."

"But where am I? Where is this place, and how are you here?" Rattler mumbled before stopping and trying to understand if this was reality or a dream. On the one hand, he felt immediately safer now that his old friend from the Wallbangers was here, but on the other hand, it created more questions than it gave answers, and his head began to hurt. He tried to close his eyes to control the pain in his head, but it didn't seem to help.

"Listen, brother, I understand that nothing makes sense right now." Clipper moved closer to the bed and sat down on the edge. "There are a lot of things you will need to be brought up to speed on, and it will take time. Your recovery from that ejection is the most important thing right now. Taking care of your health and getting you back to fighting shape is our number one goal, and there is a team here that will help you do that quicker than anyplace else— that I promise you. We have to get your affairs in order, too, and that will take some time. The mission just got bigger, and you are on the correct team. That is all I can tell you now, but rest assured that the medical team here is like nothing you've ever seen before. Dude, I'm not going anywhere. They know we're close friends that go way back, and they will take extra good care of you. Once we get you back to fighting shape, we can move onto the next phase of the mission."

"You mean, so I can go back to the Warhawks? Back out to the ship?" Rattler asked.

"Man, I wish it was that simple, but you aren't going back to the squadron or the ship. Not now or ever. Things have changed, and the game is different now. The powers at work are so much bigger than you or I could have realized when we were back in the Wallbangers dealing with our crazy skipper. He was just the tip of the iceberg, my friend. Barely a cog in a much bigger wheel, frankly, and I think he knew that; and that's why he was trying to make a name for himself. I know I'm talking very vaguely here, but there is a time and a place for everything. I'm just happy you got my email and listened to my advice," Clipper explained.

"Your email?" Rattler asked.

"Yeah, the one on the ship saying that if anyone ever asked you to fly but couldn't tell you what you would fly and how long you would be gone, just say yes," Clipper answered.

"That was you?" Rattler remembered the email back on the ship, but his brain had a hard time trying to process how long ago it was. It felt like forever.

"Yeah, man. I signed it *C.* Who else would it be?" Clipper laughed. "Listen, I know it's been a while since we spoke, and time kind of got away from me after you left the squadron. Let's be honest. Seeing our skipper go out like that took its toll on everyone. The place really wasn't the same after you left, and that's honestly a good thing, even though it doesn't sound like it. I left shortly after you did and went on to my next assignment. Test pilot school."

"Yeah, I remember hearing that. You did the lead stuff on the E-2D Hawkeye in-flight refueling, right?" Rattler asked.

"Yes, sir. That was my project." Clipper laughed. "I will forever be cursed by Hawkeye pilots of the future who have to midair refuel that beast. That seems like forever ago, man. And then one day, a guy came to me and asked me if I wanted to fly with him. He couldn't tell me how long I would be gone and what I would be flying, but you know me, bro. I love adventure, so I said yes. The rest, as they say, is history. I've been here ever since, and I do not regret the decision one bit. This is some cutting-edge tip-of-the-spear shit that rocks!"

"Where is 'here,' exactly?" Rattler asked.

"Well, that's the thing," Clipper said quietly as he looked around the room. "I can't tell you any more than I have, and frankly, I have probably already told you too much. It will all make sense when we can get you out of this room and somewhere more secure to chat. You have to trust me on that, bro."

"I do," Rattler replied somberly, wanting to know more.

"Okay. Well, I have to run right now and catch a flight. Last check before I'm helicopter qualified," Clipper replied, walking to the door.

"Wait. Helicopter qualified?" Rattler asked.

"Dude, you are going to love this place, but strap in because you are in for one hell of a ride." Clipper smiled as he left the room, and Rattler found himself alone again. Alone with his thoughts and questions. With each one that entered his brain, more pain ensued, and before he knew it, he was exhausted just trying to catch his breath. He laid his head back, closed his eyes, and tried to make sense of it all.

After some time, he gave up and decided to try to get up. He was able to get his feet on the cold floor and brace himself to try to stand.

The first attempt was not successful, and he found himself sitting again, completely exhausted. It was like his body was not his own. The last thing he remembered was when he was in the jet pulling G's and trying to evade the surface-to-air missile (SAM), and now he could barely will his legs to work. He sat on the end of the bed in the room with no idea where he was or what was going on, and he felt despair wash over him. He felt helpless and useless. He wondered what Clipper meant about not going back to the ship or back to the squadron. It didn't make any sense at all. Clearly, he survived the worst part, and he would be sent back to the Warhawks or at least back to Lemoore to wait until they finished their deployment.

Back to Lemoore meant back to Sandy and maybe a somewhat normal life. He daydreamed about their talk of him getting out and moving on to fly for the airlines and having a more stable life so that they could explore their relationship and hopefully watch it grow into something long-term. He needed to be healthy to get home to her. She would have heard about a downed Navy Hornet pilot, and she would worry. He felt her close in his heart, and it drove him to stand. Taking inventory of his body one more time, he determined it was working; it was just sore as hell, and he felt fatigued. He had to man up, get better, and get back to his woman.

He gripped the side of the bed, and with his feet firmly on the floor, summoned all his strength to stand. He would accept nothing less. The muscle fibers in his legs started to fire and awaken from what seemed to be a very long nap. As he gained his balance, it was like his brain was seeing clearly and focusing more on the task at hand—a task he could accomplish, but his body was just not used to it. It was almost like he had been in that bed forever, and he had to train his body to work again.

Slowly and steadily, he stood straight up. His joints ached, and his muscles screamed; but that pain was telling him things were working. On a roll now, he saw the window and decided to go for it. Slowly, with one foot in front of the other, he made his way to the window. Almost losing his balance many times, he finally made it and pulled back the blinds, hoping to reveal a hint about where he was. The sight that greeted him immediately told him everything was different. His life wasn't as he had known it anymore, and his brain couldn't process it at all. He heard the door open at the far end of the room, and as he turned to look, he saw a beautiful, dark-haired woman enter, and then everything went black.

CHAPTER THIRTY-ONE

"I told you he was stubborn," Rattler heard as he tried to open his eyes.

"You did say that, but this is crazy after everything he's been through. He needs rest and recovery," a female voice replied. Rattler tried to make sense of it all, but he couldn't place the voice. As his eyes opened, he saw the most beautiful woman he had ever seen staring down at him. Her combination of olive skin, dark hair, and green eyes left him speechless.

"I told you he would be okay," Clipper said. "Doc, meet Rattler. Rattler . . . Doc."

Rattler was met with the most beautiful smile beaming down at him. "Hi. You really gave us a scare there. In fact, you've given us quite a few scares over the past couple of months," Doc said.

"Hi, ma'am. Nice to meet you," Rattler replied. "Did you just say, 'past couple of months'?"

"Yeah, bro. It's time to get you up to speed. How are you feeling?" Clipper asked.

"Better," Rattler said with some hesitation. "Much better. Actually. What's going on?" He smiled at Doc.

"Listen, if Doc here clears you, we can go for a little walk, and I can explain it all," Clipper replied.

"He's good," Doc said, winking at Rattler. "Just take it easy."

With that, Doc left the room, and Clipper helped Rattler get out of bed and tossed him a flight suit that had been sitting in the corner. It fit Rattler perfectly, but it was different from any other he had worn before. The material was softer, more comfortable, yet had a tactical feel, and it was void of all patches. No rank, insignia, or patches. After he finished lacing up the boots Clipper had given him, Rattler followed Clipper out the door and down a narrow hallway that looked like a combination of a medical facility and an office building. They quickly came to an elevator. Once inside it, Clipper punched in multiple codes, which revealed a panel allowing access to floors not available when they first got in. Clipper smiled as he punched the bottom button. At this point, Rattler realized he was along for the ride, but he trusted his friend, and for the first time in a while, he felt safe.

"So, when are you going to fill me in?" Rattler asked as they exited the elevator into a series of hallways.

"We're getting there, and I'll be able to fill you in soon," Clipper replied. "Just remember, man, the truth isn't always all good."

Rattler thought about that statement and also how much Clipper had changed since the last time they were together. He was still himself at the core, but he had matured or something. Rattler couldn't put his finger on it, but it seemed his friend had been through a lot, and most of it after Rattler left the Wallbangers. As they reached the end of the hallway, Clipper stopped in front of a door, punched in some more key codes, and entered the first small room. On the left was a shelf with small bins, which Rattler could tell were for personal items since Clipper put his cell phone in one. He briefly looked to Rattler to do the same, but then he remembered that Rattler wasn't carrying anything. Once he was done, he punched more codes into a door and opened it. This gave them access to the main room, which was surprisingly big and full of life. Computer screens hummed, and about a dozen people went about their business without even giving them much of a second look. In fact, no one noticed them except for one large man in the corner.

He was a mountain of a man with bright blue eyes and a full beard. The creases in his skin and scars told Rattler that this was a man who had seen things more than a few times, that the average American couldn't even imagine. There was something about him that stood out. Even with his gruffness and hard exterior, Rattler could immediately tell this man had a huge heart just by the look in his eyes. As he looked at Rattler, he showed the caring and understanding of a lifelong friend, even if for all Rattler could remember, this was his first time seeing the man. The man half nodded and smiled at Rattler and went back to work on the computer.

Rattler followed Clipper into a smaller room off the main one as he tried to piece everything together. In some aspects, Rattler had seen it all before—the secret spaces and special protocols to enter briefing and planning areas. But in another sense, this was very different from the Navy. Everything seemed so perfect and expensive, with state-of-the-art technology and the focus on being the best that it could be, whereas in the Navy, it seemed they were always working with yesterday's technology and doing more with less.

As they entered the smaller office, Clipper motioned for Rattler to sit while he shut the door. A few last key code punches and the door locked, and a white noise machine slowly came to life. It was designed to block out any of the noise coming from outside the room, or possibly make it impossible for anyone outside to hear the conversations inside. Rattler could tell this was extremely serious because in his experience, the amount of security protocols they had gone through to get to this point was intense, and to still have two additional layers of security from the dozen or so people outside meant whatever Clipper was working on was definitely on a level Rattler never experienced. As he sat in his seat, the look on Clipper's face told Rattler he was going to hear some bad news.

Chapter Thirty-Two

Clipper paused for a moment, almost as if he were looking for the words to say.

"Come on, man. It can't be that bad," Rattler said.

"I wish that was true, buddy," Clipper replied. "This is going to be a lot, but we've known each other for over a decade. I'm just going to lay it out for you as plainly as I can and in the same way that I would want to hear this from you if the roles were switched. If you need a break at any point, just tell me and I'll stop, okay?"

"Sure thing," Rattler replied, feeling an immense weight on his shoulders.

"So, our old skipper was just the tip of the iceberg. There are two driving forces at play here that some would look at as good versus evil. They all work in the shadows. Our old skipper was a pawn for the evil side, and regardless of everything he did, he was still a small figure in a much bigger plan. I wouldn't be surprised if he didn't even know the man who was pulling the puppet strings.

"The problem is when you neutralized the skipper, you got the attention of the puppet master," Clipper said as he slid an eight-by-ten glossy photo of an old man across the desk. "This is the puppet master of sorts for the evil side. This man and his group work behind the scenes to make sure that our country is in a seamlessly endless war somewhere on the planet—all so he can fund his own personal bank account and ego. Skipper was trying to become a main player for him in the airborne early-warning and command and control aspect of the bigger picture."

"Okay, so who runs the other side?" Rattler asked.

"Good question. Everything you have seen here is run by a man you have already met, whether you remember it or not, and frankly, this is just a small part of a bigger operation. We got word that you were on the radar of Princeps Novus, and they were looking for payback for you killing Maddox. From that moment on, every move you made, every email or phone call you sent, and every flight you did was tracked." Clipper slid a photo of Rattler and Sandy together in port. It brought Rattler back to a time with her he had almost forgotten, but Clipper quickly snapped him back to reality. "So, we knew the plan for your flight with Toad was all an attempt to get rid of you. The SAM shoot down was supposed to be revenge for our skipper's demise, but it didn't work. You're too good of a pilot," Clipper said with a smirk.

"Well, not really, because I *did* get shot down," Rattler replied.

"Correct, you did, and that is where our organization jumped into action. A quick reaction force was sent out to recover you, and frankly, dude, you were in bad shape. You could have been left out there to die, but Mr. Gray ordered us to bring you back and spared no expense to get you the medical help you needed," Clipper explained.

"Mr. Gray?" Rattler asked.

"Yes, Mr. Gray is the head of this side of this war. He is the good side, the entity that does the things that the government won't or can't do, and he also focuses on keeping any evil at bay. You met him in your first medical room. The man who asked you if you wanted to fly something but said he couldn't tell you the details. Well, you answered correctly, which is why we are talking. Otherwise, you wouldn't be here right now," Clipper continued. "But you are, and it's time to focus on finishing this war and getting back to business. You pissed in the wrong backyard, and now they will not stop until they win, but there is good news."

"What's that?" Rattler was almost afraid to ask.

"They think you are dead," Clipper answered. "A body was found at the crash site. So, the other side has won as far as they know. You were reported killed in action, and everyone has moved on."

The color drained from Rattler's face, and he immediately felt sick and light-headed. Clipper handed him a bottle of water and waited until Rattler seemed to recover.

"What about my parents?" Rattler asked.

"They are taken care of," Clipper said after clicking some key-strokes and turning the computer monitor toward Rattler. A feed came into focus and Clipper zoomed in. Rattler recognized the house as the one he grew up in. Zooming in more, he could see his parents sitting on the back deck next to each other in conversation. "There was a fake life insurance policy that was paid out to them, and they will not have to worry about money ever again. They were obviously heartbroken, but they are safe. In fact, twenty-four hours a day, seven days a week, there is a quick reaction force ready to come in and protect them if the other guys try to do anything stupid. Honestly, though, I think that threat is all but gone now. Once they found out you died, the old man and Princeps Novus went back to focusing on their goals and assets. You were just a bug they needed to crush."

Rattler stared at the image, trying to soak it all in. His mom and dad seemed happy from what he could tell from the drone footage, which was surprisingly clear, and Rattler's mind moved on to trying to process the bigger picture. Then it hit him.

"What about Sandy?" Rattler asked.

Clipper looked down at the floor for a moment and then focused back on Rattler. "Maybe you need a stronger drink."

CHAPTER THIRTY-THREE

Clipper sat back down after pouring each of them a drink on the rocks.

"To lifelong brothers, those we have known and lost and those still close," Clipper said as the two raised their glasses and took a sip. "Now this part is going to hurt, but I'm here, man. Let me explain."

Rattler sat patiently and listened as Clipper explained what had progressed since he had ejected from the Hornet over Afghanistan. Rattler was shocked to learn that two months had passed, and he had been in and out of a coma during that time. They had moved him a few times over the course of the two months to get him the medical treatment he needed, but now he was good to go. Sure, it would take some time for him to get back to 100 percent, but overall, he was no worse for wear than if he hadn't ejected.

Then came the hard part. The part about why Rattler wasn't going back to his squadron or his ship.

"Okay, buddy, I know this has been a lot, and I can stop now or keep going. It's up to you," Clipper said.

"Keep going," Rattler said with very little expression. He sensed his life was going to be very different now and likely wouldn't return to what he had known in the past. It didn't matter how long he prolonged the inevitable. It was happening regardless.

"Okay, so the group that our old skipper was a part of is known as Princeps Novus, which is Latin for 'new ruler.' They are a group with a long history that essentially works behind the scenes to keep the world's nations at odds to line their own pockets. What we saw in the Wallbangers was just scratching the surface, but from everything we can tell there, it is a large contingent with roots at the Naval Academy dating back to the early nineteen hundreds. Originally, leaders got together to lead and run the midshipmen. Their bond grew as they left and had families and careers and became more and more influential. They have ties to every branch of the military and government and are deeply connected to most, if not all, military contractors that supply the weapons and aircraft that we use to fight today's wars.

"They started with honest roots from everything I can tell, but that has long since changed. The current leader is an old man by the name of Ronald Daggett. He was a naval officer and the son of Admiral Daggett. Ol' Ronny didn't do as well as his father and left the Navy early, but he followed in his father's footsteps with the Princeps Novus. But the organization has changed with him at the helm. As far as our intel indicates, prior to Ronny taking over, the overall goal of the group was to keep New World order; and, for the most part, it did things to keep the United States on the good side. Seems after this guy took over, and even more so after his father died, he took the group into the dark ages with the goal of power and money.

"His connections and network quickly shifted to the black market—primarily weapons, including biological and chemical. He seems to have a special place in his heart for unconventional warfare and likes to see people suffer. Money does not seem to be his focus. He's a devious and dangerous man who will use whatever force necessary to eliminate any threat he deems will get in his way." Clipper paused.

Rattler laughed to himself. His longtime friend was describing a person of obvious great power who was a great threat to them, but he only referred to him as "Ol' Man" or "Ronny" as a way of somewhat lessening this man's threat.

"Okay. Great, man, I get it. Our old skipper worked for this guy or in his network, but what does that have to do with me not going back to my squadron?" Rattler asked.

"I was just getting to that, man. Our intel found information that someone inside your squadron was also a member of Princeps Novus, and it is possible that your Hornet being shot down was a direct result of them trying to eliminate you," Clipper replied.

"What? Dude, this is all over. Our old skipper is dead, and I've moved on. I got my transition to Hornets and moved all over the country. No one at my current squadron knew me as a Hawkeye guy, and I've worked hard to move on from my past. There has been nothing that would even make me think that the past has caught up with me." Rattler searched his memories of the past for answers.

"I'm sorry, buddy. Intelligence has also found out that Cheri was an operative for the group and was sent to gain information on our skipper from the inside. Kind of like a double cross. That's why she basically disappeared. She was found dead in Shanghai about six months ago. Killed execution style in a hotel room. Very similar to our old squadron mate," Clipper explained.

"Shit, man. I'm really sorry about that. I know you liked her. Sorry, buddy," Rattler said.

"It gets worse. Princeps Novus tried to get to you through their mole in your squadron. From our files, we saw you had quite a bad night-carrier launch where you lost all of your electrical system," Clipper said.

"Yeah, how did you know about that?" Rattler asked.

"Dude, come on. Can't you trust that we know a lot more than you could even imagine? There are two huge forces at work here that we could never have imagined when we were Hawkeye pilots. At any rate, the next part is really going to hurt, and I want you to know that after everything we've been through and an even stranger sequence of events that has transpired, I am here for you, for whatever you need. You understand that, right?" Clipper asked.

"Yeah, man. I got it. What else do you have to tell me? Stop beating around the bush and get to it," Rattler said.

"When you somehow survived that catapult shot and recovery aboard the ship, Ol' Man Ronny wasn't happy, and he went for the next thing he could think of to hurt you. They got to Sandy, bro. Sandy is dead."

The words hung in the thick air. Rattler's world sank. His heart rate increased as he began to sweat and his eyesight focused straight ahead, but in a strange change from his past, his mood didn't fall to helplessness or despair, but to a world of anger.

"I'm really sorry, buddy—I am. But there is good news," Clipper continued. "You are dead. As far as the group and the old man are concerned, you died on a hill in Afghanistan. If and when you are willing and ready, we can use that to our advantage to take the fight to their front door. While there is a bigger picture of national security here, it is not lost on Mr. Gray that revenge is also in order. He is an honest man but also a loyal one who understands that actions have consequences, and he is willing to bring the brunt of those consequences to those involved."

CHAPTER THIRTY-FOUR

Rattler sat in a state of mild shock after asking Clipper to give him a moment. Clipper had logged into the security computer at the desk, then left Rattler to himself. On the screen were multiple windows of files that all confirmed what Clipper had explained, as well as a live feed from the security drone over his parents' house in New Jersey. No one was outside, but he stared at the screen and remembered his childhood and growing up in a small community. Life was so much simpler back then, but all of that was gone now. Never did he think his life would end up this way. Now there was only one thing on his mind. One goal that he would focus all of his energy on. The blood that ran through his veins felt colder now as his world had been thrust into this new realization, and the only thing that mattered was revenge.

He completely lost track of time as he sat in the room and processed his thoughts. His life as he knew it would never be the same. Growing up, his father always taught him to be fair and kind, but he also instilled the idea of payback when warranted. Rattler's thoughts wandered to his time with Sandy and how he would never see her again, how he had missed her funeral and his own.

A soft knock on the door brought Rattler back to reality. He turned as the door opened and the large, bearded man he saw before slowly entered. He was a mountain of a man in stature. He had the eyes of a man who had seen a lot and felt a great deal of pain, but also who would never waver until the job was done.

"Sir, may I have a moment?" the man asked in a quiet voice that didn't match his size.

"Yes, come in," Rattler replied, realizing his voice was dry from not talking.

"Sir, my name is Alexander Aleskeevich, but you can call me Brutus. That's what everyone calls me," Brutus started. "Mr. Clipper told me what happened to you, and I am sure you are hurting right now. I was wondering if I could tell you a story from my past to offer some help?"

"Of course, and I am Rattler."

The man grinned a massive toothy grin at Rattler's response.

For the next twenty minutes, Brutus went on to recall the events of his childhood in Russia, where corrupt government leaders went against his family and eventually killed his mother, father, and two brothers. Brutus was the only one to escape and had survived on his own ever since. Traveling the world, doing odd jobs, and working in mercenary positions for various wars, Brutus had seen more than any man should ever see and felt much greater loss than anyone could imagine. He went on to explain how Mr. Gray found him wounded in Afghanistan in a makeshift tribal medical facility while he was fighting the Taliban-controlled areas in the northern mountains.

"He asked me where my home was," Brutus continued. "I have not known a home since I was a child, and I told him so. He then asked what I was doing there fighting, and I told him that since I lost my family, I dedicated my life to fighting for good, for the underdog, and I'd always tried to live my life on the side of right. It was then that he took me under his guidance, much like he did you after your ejection. You may not remember, sir, but I was the one who got you out of there. I know that Mr. Gray and Mr. Clipper are far smarter than I am, but my orders were to bring you home, and that's what I did. You were in bad shape, sir, but no one was getting to you unless they went through me."

"Thank you," Rattler mumbled, trying to hold back his emotions.

"There is no need to thank me, sir. There was a connection between us from the start. Mr. Clipper told me what they did to your girl, and I volunteered for the mission. Anyway, I know I have taken a lot of your time, but I wanted to let you know that I understand your pain, and if you need anything, I am here for you. I may not be the smartest person around here, but I am very practical, and I can figure out damn near anything that needs to be done. Not to mention, this place has a lot of cool toys to play with if you are into that sort of thing." Brutus grinned as he stood to leave.

"Brutus, thank you for getting me off the ground and also for coming in here," Rattler said as he stood to shake the man's hand. "I have a lot to process right now, but I feel like you and I are going to do some good work around here in the future."

"Sir, it would be an honor to serve shoulder to shoulder with you. We will avenge your losses, but remember what you still have." Brutus looked over Rattler's shoulder at the computer screen.

Rattler turned to see someone on the back deck of his parents' house. He sat down at the computer and tried to zoom in on the video feed. It was his father standing outside, just looking at the backyard. Rattler had seen him do this since he was a child. It was his way of thinking through and processing everything he was dealing with. Rattler wished he could see his face, but the drone was directly overhead. After a few minutes, his father looked directly up, almost as if he knew the drone was there, which was impossible given the technology Clipper had described earlier. Staring at his father momentarily startled Rattler, but as he watched, his father continued to look straight up and then simply nodded before turning and walking back inside and out of sight.

Rattler knew immediately what had to be done. He wanted his life back, or at least the parts of it he could salvage. The only way he'd see his parents again was to take down Princeps Novus, and he wouldn't stop until that was done.

Chapter Thirty-Five

The following month was a blur of activity for Rattler. It was much like checking into a new squadron, but in essence, he was checking into a new life. Brutus was right about the toys to play with as well. As Clipper took Rattler around the facility, he learned that this was one of multiple bases around the world. The locations of each were on a need-to-know basis, but this was the second largest base for Mundus Tutor, or loosely translated, the World Protector. He was now a part of the other side of this underground war that no one would ever read about in the headlines, and that was, in fact, doing more work than all the levels of the department of defense combined.

A lot of their success could be attributed to the fact that there was zero red tape. Mr. Gray and the lineage of protectors that he came from acted as the board of directors that provided assets around the globe at a moment's notice to defer, defeat, and eliminate various threats. Walking through the hangar at the base, Rattler could see everything from Pilatus PC-12 transport and sensory aircraft to so many variants of helicopters that Rattler could not possibly know them all. While in the Navy, he was never good at remembering all the different types of aircraft and just tried to focus on the one he was tasked to fly, but he realized this place would be very different. Every operator went by their call sign only, except for Mr. Gray, who was only addressed as such when you saw him, which was rare.

The checkout process was quick for the pilots because each already had an extensive background flying the particular aircraft they were assigned to or flying ones so similar that it really didn't matter. This wasn't formal military training either. This was making shit happen and getting it done type of training. Rattler was shown the armory, checked in with all the various intel branches of the organization, and was given compartmentalized access to what he needed to know. The ammunition and guns would make a gun enthusiast feel like they were in heaven, and, at any time, Rattler could walk in, check out any weapon, and go shoot. That is . . . when he wasn't flying.

First came the Pilatus, which was a dream. It was outfitted with the latest in technology and sensors, but from a flying standpoint, it had the ability to fly in every type of weather, shoot any approach, and land anywhere day or night, normally or using Night Vision Goggles (NVGs). It was like a slightly smaller, much more advanced Hawkeye with way more comfortable seats. Rattler loved it. As he stood in the hangar after his latest flight, marveling at how easy it was to fly and its capabilities, he heard someone approach from behind.

"Ready to step up to the big leagues?" Clipper asked.

"Big leagues?" Rattler asked, looking around to see what could possibly outdo what he was already flying. It had been a month since his talk with Clipper, although honestly, it felt like a few days. His days were long and busy but very rewarding, as he knew they were working toward a goal to take down the organization that was responsible for so much death and despair.

Clipper motioned Rattler to follow him to an adjoining hangar, and as the two friends walked side by side, Rattler couldn't help but notice the maturity and change in Clipper. It was as if during his time in the Navy he wasn't challenged enough, which had caused him to phone it in and half-ass things when he wasn't bucking the system, almost like a kid who was too smart for the class. But in his new role, he thrived and moved with the dedication and tenacity of a man on a mission.

They exited the hangar and approached another that Rattler hadn't been in before. Clipper paused and turned around, and with a smirk, he said, "Are you ready to meet the last plane you will ever fall in love with?"

With that, he opened the side door to the huge hangar and stepped inside, allowing Rattler to follow. What Rattler saw made him speechless. Four OV-10 Broncos painted in all black sat on the hangar floor. It was clear to Rattler that these were no relics but completely restored, upgraded, and enhanced versions of the famed aircraft that was so critical in wars of the past. For an airplane thought up by two marines decades before, these showed nothing of their original heritage. Rattler took in every inch of the aircraft as he walked around them in silence. On the one hand, the aircraft was ugly compared to the Hornet, or even the Pilatus that he had been flying, but on the other, there was something about it that drew his interest. Maybe it was that he started his career flying somewhat ugly propeller planes, or maybe it was that these aircraft were far more unique than any he had seen before. He could tell very quickly that, in some regards, the technological equipment was superior to the last fighter he flew. Obviously, a multirole aircraft, these sat with various loadout stations that looked as if they could quickly be adapted and put into service with little work.

One of the things Rattler had noticed almost immediately was the lack of people at the facility. As he integrated into Mundus Tutor, he noticed many times how efficiently things seemed to work. In the Navy, there were always a lot of people involved in every situation and a constant turnover of individuals. Everyone was always being trained in everything, but it seemed different here. In fact, he seemed to almost be the only person training, while everyone else already knew their job and did it with little to no supervision. He guessed that was the advantage of a smaller dark-ops organization that didn't live in the red-tape world of Washington, DC.

"So, what do you think?" Clipper asked.

"I mean, I know what it is, but these are not like any version I have ever seen before," Rattler replied.

"Well, I know you are not much of an aircraft system guy," Clipper joked, obviously poking fun at how he had gone off to test pilot school while Rattler chased his dream of flying fighters. "I won't bore you with the details, but suffice it to say, these are very different from the original variants. The fuselage has been strengthened to be able to carry more ordnance or cargo; the engines have been upgraded to provide even more power, which is frankly not necessary, and the avionics are state-of-the-art compared to the steam gauges these came with. You can talk to or listen to anyone, take off and land damn near anywhere, and carry enough weapons to fight yourself into or out of any fight worth fighting. You are going to love flying this thing, man . . . Trust me."

"Sounds great!" Rattler replied. "When do I start training?"

The door to the back of the hangar opened, and three men came through wearing all black and carrying enough weapons to outfit a Navy SEAL team. Rattler recognized the last man as Brutus.

"How about now?" Clipper said. "We're about to leave, and I have an open back seat."

CHAPTER THIRTY-SIX

"I can't even hear the engines," Rattler said over the ICS to Clipper in the front.

"Welcome to the world of black ops, my friend. Whisper-quiet engines mean we can fly this thing into and out of anywhere without being heard," Clipper replied.

Rattler was awestruck in the back of the plane as they taxied out to the runway, which was attached to the facility. The Bronco had the feel of an old plane but was completely redone with new parts. Much like the idea of the restomod cars that he dreamed of building one day but for an aircraft. He also couldn't help but notice that even with himself and Clipper and three grown men stuffed in the very small cargo compartment, the plane felt like it wanted to jump off the ground. The performance of this thing had to be amazing.

It didn't take long for him to find out, as Clipper turned the Bronco onto the runway and, without a word, brought the power up and released the brakes. They were operating on NVGs on a blacked-out runway in the middle of nowhere. They were airborne in seconds, and Clipper went about navigating to various programmed waypoints on the display. Rattler had the same display in the back, and he could tell what Clipper was doing, even though he kept a running commentary. He joked that this was Rattler's familiarization flight and that he better pay attention because the training would be fast-paced since they needed Rattler up to speed for an upcoming mission in the near future.

At this point in his aviation career, Rattler took to aircraft pretty easily. He had been through a lot of training thus far, and there are fundamental skills that apply to any aircraft. So, once you learn how to start and taxi a plane, the rest comes quickly. He wouldn't be perfect, but he was confident that he would pick up flying the Bronco rather quickly. As they cruised along in near silence, Rattler and Clipper went over the basics of the plane—things he needed to know to not rip the wings off and how to get from point A to point B safely, or relatively so. The avionics were easy to navigate, and before he knew it, Clipper went into mission mode. Very little, up to this point, seemed like a real mission, but Clipper said it was time to get serious. He pushed a green button on his right and waited for a second green light. That was his signal to Brutus and his friends that they were close and to get ready.

"Now this might get a little rough, so . . . well, hang on!" Clipper said as he nosed the plane into the darkness. Rattler couldn't see much at all in front of them, even with the NVGs, but then it came into view: five to six infrared (IR) marker lights in a straight line. Nothing around other than that.

"Um, bro, what are you doing?" Rattler asked.

"Landing," Clipper said matter-of-factly.

Before Rattler could say anything else, the aircraft slowed, and the gear came down. Seconds later, they touched down and came to an abrupt stop. In fact, other than a carrier landing, Rattler had never stopped so quickly in an aircraft. He could hear the whine of the hydraulic cargo door open as, seconds later, the three men in black passed the right side of the plane to head off to their mission. Being last in line, Brutus gave Clipper and Rattler his signature "hang loose" signal as he disappeared into the night. In less than a minute, Clipper turned the Bronco around and took off before Rattler really could process what happened.

After a few more minutes, it was clear to Rattler that they were out of harm's way. Clipper's voice came over on the ICS. "You doing okay back there, bro?"

"Yes," Rattler replied.

"Welcome to your new life. I told you that you would love this plane." Clipper laughed.

CHAPTER THIRTY-SEVEN

"So, what was the mission?" Rattler asked.

"Capture, kill . . . standard ops, honestly," Clipper said. "It's almost funny how much time a simple mission in the air wing would take us to plan, but these guys just need a waypoint and a target, and that's it. That's why our job is so important. They need to know that we can get them in and out quickly, or at least in, like this mission. Once they are done with the mission, they will gather intel on the way home. In a day or two, we will get a call and one of the AH-6 Little Bird helicopters will go in and get them wherever they are."

"Just like that, huh?" Rattler asked.

"Yeah, man. When there is a power struggle between good and evil, there isn't any time to get caught up in the minor details. Get the mission done and move on to the next. It's the only way to make progress," Clipper exclaimed.

With that, he was off to his next thing, whether it was a mission or intel or something else. While Rattler didn't see Mr. Gray much, it seemed as if Clipper worked very closely with him. He guessed that Clipper had come on as an operator in the beginning, and now his role had expanded into more of a leadership one as well. It suited him well, and Rattler was happy about that. Before Clipper left, he explained the incredibly short checkout process for Rattler to get up to speed on the Bronco, which they would complete in the next week or so. Most flights would be tied to real missions when they could. Clipper was moving on to primarily flying the Little Bird, which he was enjoying quite a bit, and he knew Rattler would love the OV-10 because it was a mix of the prop flying of the Hawkeye and the hair-on-fire flying of the Hornet. He wasn't wrong.

Rattler went to his living quarters after the flight. Sparce as they were, they were perfect for a guy who really didn't have anything. As he entered the room, he walked past the full-length mirror. He caught his own reflection and stopped. He barely recognized himself standing there. His hair was much longer, and he was working on a weeklong beard of sorts. Not because he was trying to grow it, but because he didn't find the need to shave every day like when he was in the Navy. While an amateur might think that he wore the same flight suit, this one was actually a two-piece design that made it easier to carry various weapons. In the OV-10, there was actually a place for a rifle of sorts. When they were checking out with the armory, Brutus recommended the Sig M400 Switchblade, which Rattler enjoyed shooting, so he went with it. Additionally, he carried a Sig P226 Zev with a threaded barrel and ROMEO1 PRO sight. He loved shooting that gun; back in his previous life, he'd dreamed of owning one. When he was at the armory, he saw it and asked Brutus about it. Brutus smiled and handed him a brand-new one and two hundred rounds of ammunition to "warm up the gun with," and that was it. Rattler was definitely living in a different world, and so far, most aspects of it suited him well.

He sat down at his desk, logged into his secure computer to study some of the systems of the OV10, and pulled up the drone feed from his parents' house. Everything looked normal for a suburban house in New Jersey. His dad's truck was in the driveway, and it looked as if nothing had changed from when he was in high school. Rattler closed his eyes, his mind drifting back to that house.

While it wasn't a huge house, it was plenty big enough for his parents, his sister, and him. It had a decent-sized backyard with a small pool and deck. The neighborhood was safe, and the backyard was bordered by a train track. To this day, Rattler could sleep through the noise of a train passing by, and it likely helped him sleep on the aircraft carrier as well. The one-level house had a full basement, three-quarters of which was living space. The other quarter was his father's workshop. When he wasn't working on cars, Rattler's dad liked to spend his time woodworking, and he had a nice shop to show it. He built furniture and did other projects around the house—likely because he enjoyed it, and also because it was cheaper to build or fix something than to buy new. Rattler spent many sawdust-filled nights in that workshop watching his father. He would do anything to get back there right now.

He startled himself back to reality and sat at his desk, watching the feed of his childhood home. Sadness washed over him . . . almost as if he had allowed himself to pause for too long, and now he was going to have to deal with everything that had happened to him in the last few months. Suddenly, his head was in his hands and a single tear ran down his cheek and hit the desk. With it, the rest of his emotions flowed nonstop.

CHAPTER THIRTY-EIGHT

Deployment was almost over, and Maestro sat alone at his desk in his stateroom. He never got another roommate after the "night of the incident" with Rattler, which was how it was referred to around the ship. That night changed Maestro's whole life. He no longer had the desire to be in the Navy and wanted to get home to his family as quickly as possible. He still flew his flights and even did some combat missions, but things seemed to go quiet after the incident. Another aircraft carrier joined theirs and split the missions, and to Maestro, it was like they were just going through the motions at this point, and he was ready to go home.

All of Rattler's belongings had been boxed up and sent home to his parents. The only memory left was an empty second bed and one picture Maestro kept of both of them. With only a little time left in theater, Maestro worked hard to keep his thoughts on the mission at hand. He had often heard that the last month of any deployment was by far the most dangerous because complacency would often rear its ugly head, and when you let your guard down around the aircraft carrier, bad things happened fast. He passed most days on the ship with a combination of flying and performing his duties as an LSO and seemingly always checking his emails from home.

Word had gotten out back home that Rattler had been shot down and died, and Maestro's wife was not taking it well. He figured it couldn't be easy on the wives at home because they had to keep day-to-day life going smoothly while the pilots got to stay in their element on board the ship. Both had their difficulties, but he would rather be out here than at home trying to explain to his children when their daddy was coming home and why one of his friends never would.

They had begun to plan for the homecoming back in Lemoore, and that was an exciting time for all the families. They would be making signs and planning parties, and that would pass the time for the remaining month. Meanwhile, on the ship, the last few weeks of combat missions would be flown, and then the ship would leave the operating area and start the slow steam home. This tended to be the worst part of deployment from what Maestro had heard because the flying was minimal, and time seemed to pass slowly. He and Rattler would often talk about how they could never be on a ship and not get to fly. It would be torture for sure, and Maestro figured that's how the last week would feel.

As he sat at his desk, he missed his friend. While he had only known Rattler for a short while, there was a strong connection between them, despite being two very different people. Rattler helped him get through the first part of deployment, but he also reminded him of his own mortality when he was shot down. Something never felt right to Maestro about that night, because things seemed to go back to normal so quickly. They were told that search-and-rescue operations were handled by the Air Force, and while nothing was recovered immediately, eventually, the wreckage was found and a body was discovered.

That was supposed to be the final chapter in that story, but to Maestro, it just didn't feel right. Toad went back to flying relatively quickly and didn't even seem bothered by the events, which struck him as odd. Maybe that's what happened when you do this job for too long. Maybe when you were constantly confronted with your own mortality and the mortality of those around you, it became normal. If that was the case, that was another reason to get out. Maestro never wanted to feel that cold when it came to losing a friend and squadron mate. In the short term, he'd keep doing his job and counting the days until he was home. In the long term, he knew he had to come up with an exit strategy from the Navy that would suit his family better. Additionally, he had to figure out what he was going to do in the civilian world.

Chapter Thirty-Nine

Rattler's training was going fine. He was almost fully checked out in the OV-10, and he loved it. On the surface, everything made sense, but on the inside, something wasn't right with him. He would try to stay as busy as possible and keep his mind off things, but the nightmares would come, and sleep eluded him more and more. Inside his sparse room, he would sit and try to study or plan, depending on the mission, and his mind would wander. Day and night didn't matter anymore, nor did being cut off from the world.

The only comfort he found in his room was the video feed of his parents' house. He occasionally saw them come or go or maybe work on something outside, but overall, it provided little more than letting him know that they were still safe. Of course, he knew that without the feed, because on his encrypted cell phone, he could access files that were downloaded multiple times a day from the team that was tasked with watching his parents. The amount of manpower and money put into keeping them safe without them knowing about it blew Rattler's mind. Clearly, knowing Clipper and getting involved with the organization was the only thing keeping his parents alive. If it hadn't been for Mr. Gray and his resources, his parents were likely next on the hit list. But while all seemed to be well at home, it was not inside of Rattler. It was late, but he decided to go for a walk in hopes it would clear his head or reset something, so maybe he could get some sleep.

The compound wasn't anything to write home about, but it provided everything that the men and women needed to go about their jobs. No one wanted for anything because Mr. Gray saw to it that whatever his people needed, they got. He was an impressive leader in any right and was undoubtedly the reason the organization ran so smoothly. Rattler walked alone until he found a small spot that allowed him to look out over the surrounding mountains. It was clear to him that this piece of land was chosen very carefully to be hard to find, have mostly high ground, and be able to take off or land any aircraft needed to suit the various missions they would conduct. Like a wave in the ocean, sadness crashed over Rattler. As he sat in the darkness all alone, the feeling of being completely out of control overcame him. He would never see his parents again; Sandy was gone, and his Navy career was over. Everything he had worked so hard for was gone, and no one even knew he was alive. His friends and family had moved on, and the future was just going to be one mission after another until, ultimately, he met his fate. Thoughts of having a family and being a father and husband all vanished, and while he knew he should be happy that he was even alive, none of that mattered right now.

Without much conscious thought, he reached down to his holster and retrieved his Sig pistol. He moved it to his lap and tried to control his thoughts, but he kept repeating one thing in his mind. *You can control your own death right here and now . . .* His breathing slowed as his mind processed his likely fate. He closed his eyes and pictured seeing Sandy again and being happy and free. A euphoric feeling of freedom came over him as his mind began to accept that the end was near. Just as he was finally feeling calm about his decision, he heard someone approaching. Rattler spun around to see Brutus.

"Sir, it's just me," Brutus said.

"I really need some space, man. Is there something I can help you with?" Rattler asked.

"Well, frankly, sir, I think I can help you. I understand why you are here, and I know what you're thinking. Honestly, it's a warrior's death to be in control and die fighting a good fight, but I would like to offer you something to think about. I have sat on that very rock and had to work through the same thoughts you are working through now. I know that it feels bleak and hopeless, but there is a purpose for you. You have been put in these circumstances for a reason, and it's a situation you can handle whether you realize that or not. We are making progress for good, and while none of us will be on the front-page news for our heroics, the things I see the men and women of this organization do every day are changing the world.

"I know it's a hard pill to swallow, and I know in a relatively short period of time your personal world has changed a great deal. I have seen you operate, and you are a gifted pilot. The things you can do with an aircraft are extraordinary. Your skill set is very valuable to our mission and will help us greatly, but all of that doesn't help you right now. Right now, you are feeling lost and alone because you have lost loved ones and the ability to connect with those still around. Feeling completely alone is never easy, no matter the individual, but for someone like you who thrives on comradery, it's even harder.

"There is no shame in whatever you decide here tonight as your path forward. Please, just think about my words and know that you have a family here, a purpose here, and a path forward. With that being said, it is your decision." He produced a silencer from his pocket and handed it to Rattler. "Regardless of what you decide, sir, know that I will take care of you and ensure that others don't find out the details of tonight. You will die a warrior in others' minds if that is what you choose, or you can move forward with us and live a warrior's life."

With that, Brutus shook Rattler's hand and met his gaze eye to eye in a connection Rattler hadn't felt since he awoke from his coma.

Just as quickly as he arrived, Brutus was gone, leaving Rattler sitting on a rock in a foreign land, holding his pistol and silencer. He processed Brutus's words and was impressed by how articulate he was. Despite having a formal education, or perhaps because of it, Brutus had learned life lessons the hard and unconventional way. He had every reason to take the easy way out, but he chose not to. He still fought, and because of that, Rattler's mind began to change.

While it was true that Sandy was gone; his Navy career was over, and he likely would never see his parents again, he still had a purpose and a skill set that could be put to good use in fighting evil. The people who took so much from him would do the same to others, and maybe, with his work with the organization, he could save others from his own fate.

He controlled his breathing as his mind debated the options that lay in front of him. He could attach the silencer to the pistol and end it right now, or he could fight. He could stand up and take the fight to the enemy with the energy of a person with nothing left to lose. There was nothing they could take from him that they hadn't already, and that made him especially lethal.

Rattler closed his eyes and said a prayer for help. A prayer to his great uncle, who served in World War II, whom he felt was always watching over him. A prayer asking for the answer about which path to choose. Almost immediately, an overwhelming strength filled his body, and he stood without thinking. He opened his eyes, and the same scenery that he had been looking at since he sat on the rock now looked different. He had found new resolve, and he knew that he just overcame a huge hurdle and turning point in his life. He couldn't change what he had been through and what had happened to Sandy, but he could move forward toward the fight and bring with him the full hell and fury of a man with nothing to lose. With that, he holstered the pistol and made his way back to the hangar. As he approached, he saw Brutus standing outside in the night. Rattler made his way to the door and stopped.

"I won't be needing this," Rattler said, handing the silencer to Brutus. "Any pain moving forward will be inflicted outward and with no regrets."

"It's good to have you back, sir," Brutus replied. "Keep that. It may come in handy in the future. Now let's go make them pay."

Chapter Forty

The timeline and mission planning had to be accelerated because the carrier strike group would be leaving the area of operation within a couple of weeks. The window was small, but the plan was fairly simple: use their own plan against them. As Rattler sat in the room, he remained quiet. Clipper had mentioned prior to entering that as the new guy, he should just keep his mouth shut and listen, which he was doing.

The target was a member of Princeps Novus and was integral to the distribution of classified goods to foreign weapons dealers. To Rattler, it seemed like whoever they were referring to was on the same level as their old Hawkeye skipper—someone trying to make a name for himself and essentially selling out his country and the Navy in the process. A team would be inserted in the mountains to man various SAM sites with the idea of targeting the aircraft when it came into range. It was a standard capture/kill mission, although the people in the room didn't seem too concerned with the outcome.

With the intel on this individual only referred to as the "mark," Rattler had a hard time disagreeing. The long list of classified information he had supplied the organization was staggering. Rattler sat for a moment, trying to process how an individual who took the same oath as he did could turn against his country so badly. He wondered if it was something that started small and got completely out of hand or something that was ingrained in the person for a long time, a devious soul who only looked out for himself. Frankly, the latter scared him. At his core, Rattler was a good person who looked out for those around him, but he had learned of the true ugliness in people, and it only worked to focus his resolve against those who had taken so much from him.

Rattler continued to listen to the mission briefing, which wasn't much different from others he had heard before. The difference was this was not the world he was used to in the Navy. Here, training wasn't accomplished in a bubble, but in real life. In the Navy, the powers that be tried to schedule pilots so they wouldn't be thrown into the hardest, most dynamic missions right away but rather ramped up to them.

At this point, Rattler was confident flying the OV-10 and knew enough to get himself out of most of the trouble he found himself in. Was he as proficient as when he was flying the Hawkeye or Hornet? No, but he knew that would come with time. For this mission, he would be paired with Brutus in the back seat of a single OV-10, flying overall mission backup. His job was to be airborne and ready to flex when needed, whether that was with radio communications or getting Brutus on the ground quickly to capture the mark.

Across the room, Rattler noticed Brutus listening intently, but he could see the unhappiness on his face. From their time spent together, Rattler gathered that Brutus would rather be in one of the Little Bird helicopters that were tasked with recovering or capturing the mark part of the mission. Brutus was a knife-between-the-teeth, leader-of-the-pack kind of guy, and Rattler suspected him being in a support role and further from the action was not his first choice. On the other hand, Rattler was happy to have him aboard because he knew his training and expertise would come in handy if things went wrong, and they always seemed to at some point or another.

As the brief continued, Rattler was impressed with the level of intelligence the organization had. Everything seemed to run so much smoother and more efficiently than in the Navy. The professionalism and character of the individuals in the room struck him immediately.

While he didn't know all their backgrounds, he assumed a lot were like his. Left with nothing and nowhere to go, they came here to make a difference. These were not people who left their families to go on long deployments, who waited for emails from home hoping to get a memory of what they were missing. These were people whose whole life was the mission. They had nothing else but the men and women around them. They relied on each other and knew that injury or death could be right around the corner, yet they did it anyway. The drive and determination of those in the room—and everyone he had encountered thus far—was intense.

He sat in the back of the room, shuffling through kneeboard cards that had frequencies and plans and contingency plans not too different from a mission brief in his Hornet squadron. He organized everything in a manner that served him well in the cockpit, and he made notes where he needed to, focusing on code words that likely would come into play and their meanings while listening to the intel brief. As the brief came to a close, the briefer clicked a button on the computer to advance the slide show.

"Now, for those on the ground, in order to get a positive identification, here is your mark," the briefer said.

Rattler looked up from his kneeboard cards, and his world stopped.

CHAPTER FORTY-ONE

No one in the room seemed to notice and nothing changed at all, but Rattler's mouth hung open as he gazed at a photo of the person they had been briefed on for the last hour. On the screen was an official Navy photo of LCDR Troy Kirby. While Rattler had only been part of the organization for a short time, all the missions he had participated in thus far entailed going after weapon sites or information and intel grabs, with the occasional high-value asset grab, but all of the people looked the part: your typical bearded old man who had hate in his eyes and was going to do his part to take down the infidel machine.

Staring up at his former squadron mate affected Rattler differently. He made a noise to interrupt the briefer but was given a glare from Clipper that made him realize it wasn't the time or place. Rattler's mind flooded with memories of Toad. He was trying to justify to himself that all of this must be a mistake. Sure, he dealt with his Hawkeye skipper, but that had to be a one-off and not the norm. He couldn't fathom that there were people running around in the ranks of the military who had treasonous motivations. He began to wonder if his whole life had been a lie. Was he so naïve to believe that most people were good—when, in reality, he was operating in a world that was full of people out for their own benefit?

As the brief ended, Rattler realized this wasn't a final mission brief at all but the permission planning. There was still a lot to be done to ensure it went off without a hitch. Small bird crews were leaving in the next day or so to insert operators on the ground to man the SAM sites. This mission, while complex to its core, was being run in conjunction with an intelligence grab mission, which was often the case. With limited resources, missions were often tied together, but none of that mattered, as Rattler still couldn't process what he had seen. How could a man who was supposed to be a squadron mate and leader to him be so misguided and devious? He tried to talk to Clipper but was met with a nod and a look that made Rattler realize this wasn't the time, and Clipper would find him later.

Rattler went back to his room. Walking in a daze, his mind raced as he tried to piece together the information he had been given from Clipper after he woke from his medical coma. Rattler knew there was a struggle between good versus evil going on in the dark, out of the public eye. He knew that he stumbled upon this epic war when he found out about his Hawkeye skipper and was further thrust onto the front line when he ultimately caused his skipper's demise. Additionally, he knew that, as an act of revenge, the evil group shot him down in the mountains in hopes of killing him and ending this problem once and for all. Prior to that, they went after Sandy and got her.

After he got back to his room and shut the door, he sat at his spare desk and thought about Sandy—her blonde hair and amazing smile, the time they spent together, and the hopeful future they had ahead of them. While they never really talked about it, he had dreamt of starting a family with her. He knew she would be a great mom, and he knew they could work out the distance. As he logged onto his computer, a single tear ran down his face as he tried to imagine Sandy at the end of her life, alone and in pain. He couldn't protect her, and without realizing it, his fists clenched as his sadness grew to anger. He could feel his blood pressure rise as the computer program connected. One window explained the final systems and weapons load outs on the OV-10, and the other window showed the drone feed footage from his parents' house. He was interrupted by a knock on the door.

"Yeah?" Rattler said.

The door opened, and Clipper came in. "Listen, buddy, I get it, and I wish you didn't have to hear about it this way; but you understand that intelligence changes fast, and half the war is information management. Let me get you up to speed on everything. You have to trust me here. We've been friends for a long time, and we've been through some shit together. That bond isn't lost on me. While there are very few people in the world that I give a damn about, you are my brother, and I can only imagine everything you've been through.

"I've retrieved the latest intelligence and have it here. I know you were shocked to see Toad on the screen; frankly, most of us were. We figured this was just a lucky shot to get you out of the sky that night, but it goes much deeper than that. This goes way back, and while I have no evidence to prove it, my gut tells me your orders to VFA-97 were not a coincidence at all. I think this was planned all along after our skipper took his final dance with the COD's propellers."

"You really think it's that deep?" Rattler asked.

"Well, personally, yes I do, but you know me. I have very little trust for anyone, and I never really have," Clipper replied. "I know that at their core, people can be horrible and are just looking out for themselves, so very little surprises me at this point in life. I love you like a brother, but, dude, you can be naïve. If you aren't careful, that will get you killed one day. The people we are dealing with, the ones we are fighting, have no issue with taking your life or the life of anyone around you. Collateral damage is not something they even consider because it is all about power to them. Maybe one time they cared about doing good, but it quickly changed and they became money driven. Now they have all the money they could need or want, so it is a power-driven motivation. That's when it gets scary because, unlike money, a tyrannical man can never get enough power. They will just lust for more until their end. They will lie on their death bed, breathing their last breath, wondering how they could have controlled more people and had more power. These men need to be taken out quickly and with extreme violence before they get even more out of hand.

"Take a look at this file and go over it all. It will show you how connected they are and how the SAM wasn't the first attempt on your life. The mission will happen, but if you don't want to be on it, that's fine. However, I need your head in the game on this one. Lots of moving parts, and I'm not questioning your ability, but this is your first real mission since getting here. I've got Brutus with you, and he can think on his feet, but he's not a pilot, so I need your best with that Bronco."

"Thanks, man. Sorry. Still trying to get my feet under me here, but I'll look over all this and be ready. What's the timeline?" Rattler asked.

"Ground team is tonight. I'll be flying one in. Give them a couple of days to get the lay of the land, and then it will depend on the air wing schedule. We need Toad to be fragged to come up north and get within range. The powers that be want this to be a capture and intelligence grab, but you know how these things can unravel. Be ready to go in forty-eight hours, and then we wait for our window," Clipper said as he moved to leave the room. "Dude, I get it that this is hard to process. When I came here, it was under completely different circumstances, but you wouldn't be here if you couldn't handle this."

CHAPTER FORTY-TWO

Maestro sat in the VFA-97 ready room, listening to the skipper talk to all the officers. He spoke about the final two weeks of deployment, the loss of Rattler, and how things didn't go according to the plan he had when they left San Diego six months prior. His intent was to bring all his people home, and he failed at that. Maestro could tell that the skipper was pretty beat-up about it, and it was something that would likely stick with him for the rest of his life. That's the thing about taking over a command. Regardless of what happens, the buck stops with you, and there is nothing anyone can say to change that.

The skipper had aged exponentially during this deployment, and Maestro felt bad for him. He would go home to his family and bring with him all the pain and anger from this deployment. All in all, the squadron wasn't really doing anything of merit, and if not for the loss of Rattler, the deployment would go down as a nonevent. That wasn't the case for the members of VFA-97, as they were coming home one short, and the skipper focused on that and how he needed everyone to have their head in the game for the rest of their time at sea. Once they got home, they would all get some well-deserved rest and time off, but until then, he needed them all at their best. The remaining combat missions were few and far between and would likely not amount to much, but this was the most dangerous time of deployment for everyone. Skipper tasked his officers with checking on each and every one of their men and women and making sure everyone was focused to finish this together, in one piece, and get back to Lemoore.

Maestro couldn't help but feel a little annoyed by the statement that this was the most dangerous part of deployment. He had lost his friend and roommate, and he couldn't imagine anything more dangerous than that. On the other hand, he understood what the skipper meant, and he was ready to be done. With any luck, he wouldn't have to go on any combat missions at all and would just stick to flying mundane flights around the ship. All he wanted was to get off this ship, be home with his family, and figure out what his future held. He knew one thing for sure: it would not have anything to do with the Navy. This deployment taught him that as soon as he could, he would get out and do something else. He just needed to figure out what that was.

As Skipper finished up, he held up the proposed schedule for the last two weeks. He looked a little dejected by the fact there were so few combat missions scheduled, as the other air wing had already taken over much of that duty. He mentioned that only three sections were scheduled to go into country in the next two weeks, and the rest of the daily flying would be aimed at finishing up training and upgrading flights for the pilots around the ship. This would allow for more time off when they got home. Once the carrier turned and headed home, they would stop most flight operations and just sail home as quickly as possible.

Maestro had hoped he would just do the last flight to finish up his next qualification in the Hornet and then be done. Unfortunately, as the skipper concluded his speech, Maestro learned that he would be finishing up his qualification, but he was also the last section scheduled to go into country on this deployment. He would be Toad's wingman on the last combat operation VFA-97 would do.

While he wasn't at all happy about it, he knew it was his job, and he would just focus and get it done. Maybe flying over where Rattler went down would bring some closure to losing his friend. At any rate, the finish line was in sight. Maestro and the rest of the War-hawks just needed to keep their heads in the game and finish strong.

CHAPTER FORTY-THREE

Rattler finished another day, which seemed to be a mirror image of everyday life. He would wake up early and study the OV-10. He had never learned more about a plane from documents in his life, but the flying time was limited. While on active duty, he constantly trained, but here it seemed the training was limited to a mission. At times, it seemed never-ending, but there were times when it slowed down. As the organization prepared for the next major mission, his flying was limited to low-level nighttime. There was no need to pop up on the radar of some Airborne Warning and Control System (AWACS) aircraft and gain attention when it wasn't warranted. During the day, he would spend time out on the range with Brutus, getting experience with the different weapons they would carry. While his Sig pistol and cockpit rifle were the go-to weapons that he focused his energy on, Brutus always surprised him with something fun, whether it was teaching him how to wire C4 or shoot a 50-cal machine gun. Brutus believed in being prepared for anything and everything.

As the two spent more time together, Rattler learned about his new friend's past. Even with everything Rattler had been through in recent times, he couldn't imagine the pain of having his whole family killed by members of the government. To lose everything at such a young age was something Rattler couldn't fathom. Brutus never had a childhood, never just ran around his neighborhood and played like kids do. At moments during their time together, Rattler felt guilty about his own pity party when there were people in this world who had it so much worse.

Brutus was giving Rattler so much more than the weapons and tactics training crash course. Brutus was teaching him the art of revenge—the way to harness the negative energy in life and turn it on the people who deserved it the most. If you met Brutus outside of the organization, you'd think he was a kindhearted person who would help an old lady across the street and carry your groceries to your car. He would never ask for anything in return. That's who he was to his core, but there was another side of him, a side of pain and hurt and loss that lurked below the surface. That side of him would not only kill but would also dismantle anyone who was responsible for his loss. In a way, he lived two lives, and it was very interesting to Rattler to see this. Instead of pushing down his pain, Brutus showed Rattler how to channel it toward those it should be directed at. Focus the negative energy on the enemy and unleash the full force of what you are capable of toward them. It was a way to not only prevent death, despair, and the loss of others in the future, but also to turn the negative energy inside him onto something other than himself.

As they finished up another training session and were cleaning their weapons and sharing one of the beers Brutus always seemed to be able to find, Clipper walked up. Rattler still couldn't get over how quiet the compound was. You would never hear the helicopters take off and land due to the quietness of their engines, and the PC-12 was quiet enough as well. In fact, the only thing that made any real noise was the OV-10, and they came and left so quickly that the noise was short-lived. Rattler could tell that Clipper had just returned from a mission and, likely, the drop-off of ground forces to secure the SAM sites.

As Clipper made his way over to the two, Rattler couldn't help but see how different he had become. Long gone were the days of him being a party animal, not really giving a shit about anything but finding the next good time. What Rattler saw now was a man who had aged and matured with the experience of a test pilot and now an underground operative who put his knowledge and skill set to good use. Clipper could fly anything with wings, and some things without them, but he was never challenged in the Hawkeye. In fact, to the best of Rattler's memory, the only time Clipper was really happy in the Wallbangers was when he was wrestling with a stricken Hawkeye or their treasonous leader. The rest of the time, he was bored and used his energy to seek out ways to blow off steam. That usually involved someone thin and tall who was looking to make equally poor decisions. It was only with Cheri that Rattler saw something change in his friend. He seemed more serious and committed to being himself and seeing if it could work out. He could only imagine how Clipper took the news that he had essentially been set up and that Cheri was only after information and had no real interest in him at all. That changed a man. Feeling deceived deeply changes you to your core, and maybe that was part of the difference Rattler was seeing in his friend.

"First part of the mission is complete," Clipper said as he approached. "We dropped off two teams at different sites. There will be a brief tomorrow, but the frag will be to get Toad into a valley and hit him from all sides. From what we're reading, he is quite the tactical pilot, and we don't want to risk missing him. Our two teams are the best we have."

"Thanks!" Brutus joked.

"You know what I mean," Clipper shot back. "I need you on a higher level for this one. You are the cleanup. If shit goes sideways, I know Rattler can get you on the ground and you can act as a one-man wrecking crew to get Toad back to interrogation. The focus here is to take him back and lock him up. Our hope is that if they realize we can reach out and grab their guys, they will think twice about acting with such reckless attitudes.

"These people and this organization have been working too long without real consequences. It's time to show them that the risk isn't just death, but maybe life in a really shitty prison cell. My guess is they all think they are above that, and none of them would survive very long alongside the people we intend to house them with. So, think of it as intelligence and psychological warfare, all wrapped up in one nice package. Did you finish the mission prep?" Clipper asked Rattler.

"Yeah, I've read it all more than once," Rattler replied.

"I know that shit hurts, bro, but stay focused," Clipper answered.

Rattler just nodded as he went over everything he read again in his head. Nothing happened by coincidence, and from the start, it looked like his orders to VFA-97 were set up as a way to get him close to Toad. Toad and Rattler's Hawkeye skipper were close at the Naval Academy, where they first met. Acting as Toad's mentor, the skipper brought him into the organization early, and therefore, when he heard about the untimely death of his friend, Toad was set to get revenge.

He did it from the start when he tried to befriend Rattler at the Warhawks and then sabotage his jet. It was the easiest way to get rid of him and get his revenge. What Toad didn't count on was Rattler's natural ability to handle situations when they went sideways. The last major attempt was the electrical failure off the catapult. The thought was that while Rattler could probably handle that anywhere else, he would likely screw up and fly himself into a watery grave sixty feet above the water. Most pilots would, and Rattler might have given any other night, but that night it wasn't his time. He got back aboard safely, and that's when they decided to go after Sandy. They thought hitting Rattler where it hurt the worst would cause him to self-destruct, and the problem would fix itself. It was as much about eliminating Rattler as it was about showing the power they had. Before he even knew about it, Mr. Gray and the organization stepped in and began protecting Rattler's parents. Without their knowledge, there were teams tracking them and ensuring they were not the next target. They likely would have been if fate hadn't intervened, and

Rattler hadn't become a target the night of the SAM shoot.

When Toad went to the tanker, he actually switched secure communications with forces on the ground and passed tracking information for Rattler's jet. Rattler had no chance as the SAMs launched out of nowhere, with no warning, and were already locked onto Rattler. Even the best pilot didn't stand much of a chance. Rattler's time was up. Toad was directly responsible for that and took it upon himself to save face after the electrical failure didn't work. That's where the organization stepped in and got Rattler to safety, and the rest was history.

After reading and rereading the intelligence file. Rattler grew more and more angry. This was different than before. Much like Brutus, Rattler started living two lives. There was a lot he couldn't control and a lot of feelings that would never leave him, but in the end, he knew the enemy, so he directed all of his hatred toward that target and did everything in his power to fight the enemy with the maximum lethality.

In a lot of ways, Clipper was right. LT Owens was dead and was never coming back. That life was over, but another life had begun—a life of secrecy, adventure, and the ability to finally do some real good on this planet. Not the bullshit fighting of a war that was never going to be won or lost but real-deal shit that would make a difference. Actions that would turn the tide of good versus evil and affect lives long into the future. For far too long, high-powered people made personal and financial gains using the lives of others as chess pieces. That time was over, and Rattler and the others in the organization were ready to send shock waves through their confidence. It was time that the untouchables learned that they were vulnerable.

CHAPTER FORTY-FOUR

After the team was inserted into the mountains to control the SAM sites, the rest of the crews waited. Mission intelligence briefs were held daily, and as time passed, they seemed to increase in both length and information. Mr. Gray would frequent the briefings to ensure that any changes could be decided on at a moment's notice. He was ultimately the puppet master of this show, and in his mind, he knew this could be their one chance to shift the tide of this war. He was not going to miss that opportunity. Rattler could sense the anticipation as the days drew on. Every day, the intelligence group would brief the members of the mission on whether Toad would be flying into the area of operations. Every day, it seemed as if it changed, and they were starting to suspect that Princeps Novus was on to them and were possibly trying to keep Toad safe and out of their hands. There was no telling how much intel capturing Toad would bring, and Mr. Gray was growing impatient. As the group filed into the secure briefing room, there was a different vibe in the air. Something was different, for sure. Rattler nodded to Clipper, who was very busy, and took his seat next to Brutus in the back of the room.

"You ready?" Brutus asked Rattler.

"Is it happening?" Rattler countered.

"Yes, sir. Game time." Brutus nudged Rattler's side.

This brief started off like no other Rattler had sat in. The briefers were the top-tier members of the organization, and Mr. Gray sat in the center of the first row. Clipper orchestrated things from the side of the room, and Rattler would have known from the start that it was time to go, even if Brutus hadn't told him. Kneeboard cards were passed out with frequencies and call signs. Rattler scanned down to see what his was. "Ghost," which seemed appropriate, as Rattler was about to come back from the dead. They tried to keep the mission as simple as possible. Toad's flight, call sign Hellcat 11 and 12, would be working with a SEAL team on the ground. The SEAL team's call sign was "Black Widow," and the team was made up of the members Clipper had inserted days before. They would bring the two Hornets close into the area and then fire multiple SAMs at Hellcat 11. Since they knew Toad's skill level and the proximity fuses of the SAMs, the goal was to shoot down his jet and then allow him to eject. Following ejection, the ground teams, aided by two Little Birds, would swarm in and pick up Toad for interrogation and eventually hand him over to a government agency tasked with what to do with him next. That didn't seem to be a concern for anyone in the room; their task was getting their mark. The Little Birds would be a flight of two led by Clipper in Angel 11 and a second bird flown by a pilot Rattler hadn't met before.

As he sat in the back of the room, Rattler's feelings were a mix of rage and disbelief that he was briefing a real-world mission to take down Toad—a person he had considered a squadron mate and borderline friend just a few months prior. While he was closest with Maestro, he did spend a workup cycle and most of a deployment with the rest of the squadron. His disbelief didn't last long, as the rage took over. Rattler had to believe that Clipper and the rest of the organization had good intel and weren't operating on the side of evil. Everything he had seen in his time here and the people he met reinforced this belief. Still, looking up at the corner of the briefing screen and seeing his old squadron mate's face just seemed odd.

The rest of the brief was mundane as they went over contingency plans and the backups. Rattler would be flying a sole OV-10 as a communication and mission relay plus backup grab if something happened to the Little Birds. He and Brutus would be outfitted with two AIM-9X missiles and two rocket pods. Other than that, it was just them, their personal weapons, and each other. Rattler trusted Brutus and knew he would be an asset to help him get through this mission. The only other players in the area were Hellcat 12, Toad's wingman, and Cyclops, which was the E-2C Hawkeye operating in the area.

The last brief was the ship's flight schedules and air plan. Rattler scanned to see who would be in those roles, and two names jumped out immediately. The mission commander of the Hawkeye would be Brucie. Rattler and Brucie went back to Rattler's time in the Hawkeye. She was the skipper of the Hawkeye squadron, but Rattler knew her from back in the day when she was a junior officer. Brucie was as cool as they come, and while he hadn't followed her career completely, when he reported to VFA-97, he noticed she was about to take command over at the Hawkeye squadron. She deserved it, and everyone who worked for her was working for the best skipper in the fleet. He was equally proud and nervous that she would be in the air tonight. He knew the plan didn't call for the Hawkeye to be anywhere near the ambush, but he also knew that plans could change when Mr. Murphy of Murphy's Law showed up at the wrong time. Scrolling down the screen, Rattler's heart sank again, and he felt light-headed. Hellcat 12 tonight would be his old roommate, Maestro.

CHAPTER FORTY-FIVE

"Sir, can we talk?" Rattler asked Mr. Gray after the brief ended.

Clipper was in earshot and made his way over.

"Son, are you ready for this?" Mr. Gray asked.

"Yes, sir. It's not about me. It's about Hellcat one-two. He was my roommate, and there is an issue. He can't be anywhere near the action tonight. He is a father and husband and has kids back home, sir. I couldn't live with myself if they lost their father," Rattler exclaimed.

"Well, there are always risks, but our ground crews know which Hornet to target, and I assure you we have ways of making sure we know which one is Hellcat one-one and which is Hellcat one-two," Mr. Gray answered.

"Sir, how good is the intel on the ship? What if the crews swap jets or Toad's jet breaks and he doesn't make it airborne? I need to know with 100 percent certainty that he's in the jet that is targeted," Rattler said, seeing that Clipper was giving him a look to shut up.

"Son, nothing in this world is 100 percent, and you know as well as I do that intelligence reports certainly never hit 100 percent accuracy. We operate in a world where there are risks. I have lost a lot of sleep over what Toad has done against his country. The list of lives lost because of his actions is not short. Innocent men, women, and children have been killed directly because of his treasonous action

179

against our nation to line his pockets. Frankly, just thinking about him makes me sick. While I cannot promise you 100 percent accurate intelligence, what I can assure you is I've had my best people working on this from the start. Your squadron mate is in the top tier of the hierarchy on their side and needs to be dealt with. One way or another, this has to happen. I have eyes everywhere, and we will know with the greatest certainty who will be in what jet. This is our last window to execute this mission, and we need to take it. Otherwise, all the planning and preparation will be for nothing.

"Once the jets are in the area of operation, my men on the ground are the best at what they do. With their sensors and weapons, they will be more than certain they are targeting the correct jet. All of that being said, much like you and all others who sign up for this job, your roommate knows the risks. I know that may sound cold, but it's reality. I assure you that you have lost friends in this job for reasons that are far deeper than what they appear on the surface. I take my role in this very seriously, and you need to know that I do not want any loss of life other than the intended mark.

"We will do the best we can, but I have to ask you . . . Are you ready for this? You have been through hell, and I know you are adjusting to this new life. It's easy to see the strain and stress this has caused you. There would be no foul in you taking yourself off this flight, even if you weren't so closely attached to everything that's going on. You need to remember that in the world we operate, this isn't personal. This is business, and our role in this war is to keep the values and virtues of our country intact. When you joined the Navy, you swore to defend all enemies, foreign and domestic, but I know you never thought that the domestic would be the greatest threat," Mr. Gray said.

"Yes, sir. I understand the risks and I'm ready. Frankly, there is no place I'd rather be," Rattler replied, thinking about the risk to his roommate.

"Fly safe, son," Mr. Gray answered.

CHAPTER FORTY-SIX

Rattler was left to himself as Clipper went about more mission preparations. Brutus had already left to head to the armory. He knew he was in good hands with this team, but he was still unsure if he was up to the task and wondered what he could do to ensure that his roommate would be safe. He had already lost so many people in his life in such a short time that he wasn't sure he could handle losing any more, especially someone who had so much going for him at home.

He made his way back to his room to mentally prepare and get his things together before heading to the hangar. He was confident in his ability to fly the OV-10 and enjoyed flying it more than anything else he had flown before. It was a mix of everything he had done up to this point in his life, and it suited him well. While the Hornet was a blast to rage around and pull G's, and the Hawkeye was fun because he got to fly with his friends, the Bronco was a little bit of both and more. After he preflighted his gear and weapons and ensured that his black flight suit was completely sanitized of all things that would identify him, he watched the feed from his parents' house. He knew that this organization had very deep pockets, but the idea that he could check in on them at a moment's notice still shocked him. They were half a world away, and he could zoom in and see his father sitting on the back deck, drinking a cup of coffee. He longed to be back there now or even talk to them, but that wasn't a possibility at the moment. He had to move forward knowing they were safe and that hopefully, one day, things would change, and they could reunite. For now, he had work to do.

Very little from his previous life followed him to this place, but there were a few things he kept. The first was his watch, a gift from his parents. It was a Breitling Cockpit B50 in all black, and Clipper wore the same. While it was a little beat-up, he always flew with it, and the organization didn't find any distinguishing marks, so they allowed him to keep it.

The second thing was more personal. Rattler's father was a fisherman by hobby and believed a good knife could make or break the perfect fillet. When Rattler joined the Navy and finally got his wings, his father couldn't be prouder, but before the first deployment, he gave Rattler a special knife to carry when he flew. His father understood the dangers of flying, and while the likelihood of having to bail out or eject was slim, he wanted his son to be prepared.

Rattler handled the Speedgoat knife that his father gave him as a gift. It was a handmade knife from a small company in Montana that specialized in such things. The blade was made of black carbon steel measuring 3.75" long, and no matter what Rattler did to the knife, it never dulled. The handle was wrapped in a black 550 cord that could be used in a pinch for many survival situations. As Rattler slipped the knife into the sheath, which was attached to the back of his belt on his special two-piece flight suit, he felt better knowing that if things went sideways, he would have a tool that could help him get out of anything, and if needed, a weapon he could use as a last line of defense.

As Rattler went over the mission one more time in his head, he felt ready. This part was really quite simple. He and Brutus would launch in a single OV-10 and operate on NVGs while being the overall airborne coordinator as well as the secondary—and really tertiary in Rattler's mind—option to pick up Toad after he was shot down. This was assuming that both of the Little Bird aircraft couldn't get in, which was highly unlikely. While the mission was a capture or kill, Mr. Gray emphasized that capture part in the brief. He seemed to want Toad alive for one reason or another.

All of that was well above Rattler's level of need to know, and he was fine with that. There was once a time when Rattler wanted to be involved in everything and know every detail, but as he got older and dealt with the real-world events that brought him here, he was far more content with just doing his job and keeping his head down. While every mission had its risks, Rattler felt that this one was fairly benign. They would take off and head in low to be in the proper position. He needed to be low enough not to pop up on the E-2C Hawkeye's radar, but high enough to get radio coverage to keep track of everything that was going on. In all likelihood, he would fly low while Brutus listened to various frequencies. Once Toad was taken by Clipper's team, Rattler would return to the compound and that would be it. He ensured that the Sig was loaded and ready to go and that he had two spare magazines, just in case. He thought about the men on the ground who had been lying low for the last few days and what that must be like. As a pilot, he spent very little time in that world other than his ejection, and frankly, he didn't remember much of that.

His mind shifted to Brutus and the life he had lived thus far. He always found it hard to feel bad for himself when he thought of all that Brutus had endured. Finally, his mind shifted to Maestro, his closest friend in the Warhawks, and how close to the action he was going to be tonight. He remembered Maestro's wife and what a kindhearted woman she was. Rattler had grown cold, and hatred filled his blood with everything that was taken from him; but he knew one thing for sure: He could not let anything happen to Maestro tonight. No matter what, he had to ensure his roommate made it back to the ship and back to his family.

He sat at his desk and thought about all the things he would change in his life and all the things he wished he could do over, but none of that seemed to matter anymore, as his focus was on Toad now. This man tried to kill him and was in some way responsible for him losing Sandy. A tear ran down his face as he thought about Sandy and how sweet and pure she was. The thought of her dying on the street alone only made him more focused and angrier. All of his rage was focused now. As he closed his computer feed and silently said goodbye to his parents, Rattler didn't care what happened to him tonight, but he would not let anything happen to Maestro or his team. These men had already taken far too much, and that ended tonight.

CHAPTER FORTY-SEVEN

As Rattler approached his OV-10, he noticed once again how different flying here was from the Navy. There was no plane captain to greet him and snap a salute and no maintenance personnel waiting around in case something broke. Everything was in place and ran perfectly. As he approached his black Bronco, he could see that Brutus had already completed his preflight and was sitting in the back seat. Under different circumstances, Rattler would think he was going up for a joyride with a friend, but as he looked over the sinister-looking Bronco, that was obviously not the case. This weapon of war was ready for battle.

Perfectly clean and ready to go, the Bronco held rocket pods under each wing as well as two AIM-9X missiles. Rattler never knew much about the Bronco while he was in the Navy since, as far as he knew, they stopped using them long before he joined. He had since learned that wasn't the case, but he was still surprised to learn that this machine that was designed for a multitude of roles could also hold its own in the air-to-air arena. It didn't have the radar of a fourth- or fifth-generation fighter aircraft, but if it found itself in a fight, it wasn't totally useless either.

Rattler ran his hand across the fuselage, almost talking to the plane. He had a habit of doing this when he got ready to fly. Subconsciously, it was a way to connect with his aircraft. He needed to become one with the plane to feel more connected in flight. Otherwise, bad things could happen. Satisfied that everything was set up, he climbed into the cockpit. If he had any doubt about how upgraded this aircraft was, it all disappeared when he looked at his instruments. The round steam gauges were long gone, all replaced with digital displays and multifunctional displays (MFDs) to allow him to select various menus to do anything from monitor aircraft systems to cycle through weapons selections. Additionally, the radio suite was much more advanced than that of the original OV-10.

A mix of emotions swirled through Rattler as his fingers ran over the various buttons and switches needed to prepare the aircraft for start. On one hand, he was happy that he was beginning to feel one with the aircraft. He was amazed at how quickly he had become comfortable with the plane. In a lot of ways, it was the quickest he had taken to a plane in his life. On the other hand, his rage continued to grow. While he tried to put Sandy, his parents, and Maestro out of his head, he couldn't help but think about everything that was taken from him. He had done nothing to get pulled into this world and only reacted to the circumstances of his Hawkeye squadron. The fate of his former skipper was not a result of his direct intent and was only a byproduct of his reaction to what was presented to him. Now his whole life had shifted, and he sat in a covert aircraft in a mountainous compound, waiting to take off on a mission that would never be discussed in the branches of the government, except at the highest level, to fight an enemy that was born from within. The ultimate fight between good versus evil was about to happen, and Rattler was at the tip of the spear. Lost in his thoughts, he didn't notice Clipper run up to the side of the aircraft.

"Hey, brother, one last check. You okay?" Clipper shouted.

"Yeah, man. Let's get this done," Rattler replied.

"Just remember, this is a capture/kill with emphasis on the capture," Clipper replied.

"Understood, man. Nothing personal, just business," Rattler shouted down, giving a thumbs-up.

Clipper half smiled and half rolled his eyes as he walked away, knowing that his longtime friend had far too much invested in this mission for it to not be personal.

Rattler went back to his preflight flows and checked the time on his watch. He was ahead of schedule, and as he checked the fuel level, he noted he would have plenty as long as the mission went off as it should. The Little Birds would be starting soon, not that anyone would hear their engines, and then Rattler would fire up the Bronco, taxi out, and take off. Everyone would move to their prebriefed site and get an intelligence update airborne.

Rattler knew the mission was already in motion as Toad and Maestro had likely already launched from the ship and were heading north. Their fates would meet over the same mountain range where Rattler found himself face-to-face with a SAM site of his own just months prior. This time, Rattler was on the offensive and the cards were stacked in his favor. Toad would have no idea what hit him if all went according to plan, and then he would be picked up and have to pay for his actions against his country. Rage, resolve, and focus tightened inside Rattler as he spoke into his ICS to Brutus in the back.

"Ready to start?" Rattler asked.

"Fire 'em up, boss. Time to head to the party," Brutus replied.

CHAPTER FORTY-EIGHT

The OV-10 started with ease, and Rattler taxied it right out of the hangar and onto the short taxiway. It would only be a minute or two from engine start to takeoff, and that's how the organization liked it. While they had the perimeter secured for many miles around the compound, it never hurt to be quiet and convert. The fewer eyes on them, the better. Rattler caught a glimpse of his own eyes in the mirror on the canopy bow as he looked up. Piercing blue eyes met his gaze, and he almost didn't recognize himself. In a lot of ways, he shouldn't, because the old Rattler was long dead. Gone were the days of being an innocent kid in his dad's garage or a flight student, or even beginning his first deployment with the Wallbangers. All of that was gone now. He moved the power up slightly to align his aircraft with the short runway attached to a covert base that was in the process of fighting a war that no one knew about. Gone were the women that Rattler loved, one by choice and one by the hands of the enemy. Gone were his parents, or at least communicating with them in the way that he loved. Most of all, gone was the innocence of believing that there was good in this world and that most people wanted what was best for themselves and those around them. He knew now the ugly truth: People were mostly out for their own good, and even the men and women he served with in the Navy, who above all else were supposed to be serving something greater than themselves, were trying to line their own pockets. At least, some of them were.

Once they were aligned with the runway, which would be almost impossible to see if it wasn't lined with IR lights that reflected in Rattler's NVGs, he made a quick double-click of the ICS to Brutus in the back. Brutus replied with a single click back, which was the signal that he was ready to go, and Rattler quickly pushed the throttles up and rocketed down the runway. The Bronco was fairly light with just two people aboard, even two the size of Rattler and Brutus, plus two AIM-9X missiles and two rocket pods. The idea was that the aircraft had to be ready to flex to anything that went wrong with the mission at a moment's notice. That meant minimal crew, a couple of air-to-ground and air-to-air missiles, and that was it. If they needed to land and subsequently take off from a small field or dirt area, they didn't need to worry about being overweight. They wouldn't need much gas at all because, since the compound was close to the area where Toad and Maestro would be flying tonight, it wouldn't take them long to get there. The Little Bird crews, led by Clipper, had been on alert to be ready to go and had taken off about thirty minutes ago. Now it was Rattler's turn.

So far, all the intelligence, both gathered and in real time, was on point. Both Toad and Maestro launched without incident off the ship and headed north, just as they had done many times before. Nothing was out of the ordinary, and there was confirmation of who was in each aircraft, although Rattler was still worried about his old roommate. His mind was racing, trying to come up with a way to ensure Maestro wouldn't be anywhere near the action when it went down. He had a plan, although he doubted that Mr. Gray and Clipper would be too enthusiastic about it.

As Rattler maneuvered the Bronco with ease along the route he had planned to get to his holding area, he went over the details in his head. He knew he needed to have Brutus on board with the plan he had in mind, but he wanted to wait until they were airborne and alone to bring it up.

"You up on ICS?" Rattler asked.

"Go ahead, sir. Just monitoring the intel frequency for updates. Sounds like all is going according to plan. Hellcat one-one and one-two are in the area of operations and talking to our guys on the ground. They are just holding them and having them monitor the area until everyone else is in place. The only glitch so far is Clipper is alone because the other Little Bird went down on deck for a gearbox issue. They are working a spare right now, but I know the guys on Clipper's bird, and they are the best. They will pick up Toad as soon as Clipper lands near the crash site," Brutus replied.

"Okay, man. Look, this is going to sound insane, but hear me out. I need you to get Cyclops up on the radio. I have an idea to get Hellcat one-two out of the area to ensure my old roommate is safe," Rattler said over the ICS, which was followed by silence. He knew that even mentioning this to Brutus could end up going bad for him. The organization thrived on people doing their jobs as they were briefed for the mission. They didn't need a bunch of cowboys going off script.

"Sir, you understand that if you do this, you will be over a clear frequency and risk the whole operation. They will most likely record it," Brutus finally said.

"I know that. I also know that I'm asking you to hang your neck out there. Hear me out. There are two men flying those Hornets tonight, and as evil and sinister as one is, the other is a family man with a wife and kids. If there is any chance that the guys on the ground can mix up the targeting, then there's a chance we could very quickly switch to the side of evil by shooting down an innocent man who is just trying to serve his country. Would we be any better than the others if we did that?" Rattler asked.

Of course, he was trying to play to Brutus's family side, and he knew that Brutus would understand the pain Maestro's family would feel if something happened to him. Sure, there were risks when you go on deployment, but this was different. Rattler was hoping Brutus would help him out and ensure his friend was safe. Then the rest could go according to plan. At the end of the night, Toad would be in an interrogation cell, and they could put all this behind them. If Rattler was lucky, maybe no one would even know they deviated from the plan.

"What do you want me to do?" Brutus asked.

Rattler went on to explain that he needed to get Cyclops on the radio. He knew that if he could convince the Hawkeye to change the tasking momentarily to get Hellcat one-two out of the area, there would be less of a chance of Maestro getting wrapped up in the mission. After explaining it all, Rattler finished with, "Listen, I know it's a simple idea, but I also know the skipper of that Hawkeye squadron. She is top-notch, and we go way back. While I will not specifically identify who I am, I bet she will have an idea that we know each other. She is as loyal and patriotic as they come, and if she knows that Maestro needs this tasking, then she will help. If I know anything about Brucie, I know that she loves her country and her fellow air wing crews. If she knew how involved Toad was with this treasonous plot, she would take him out herself if she could."

"Standby. I will try to work some radio magic back here," Brutus replied.

"Thanks, brother. I owe you one," Rattler said.

"Sir, let's be clear. You will owe me more than one." Brutus laughed.

CHAPTER FORTY-NINE

Rattler eased the Bronco into low orbit over his holding point as he checked the vitals of the mission and aircraft. Everything seemed to be going according to plan, other than one of the Little Birds not making it, but he knew Clipper would be able to hold his own alone. Everything on the Bronco was working perfectly, which Rattler had come to expect. The guys and girls who maintained these planes were top-notch, and he was sure that they were swarming over the other Little Bird, fixing it as he orbited. Rattler monitored the main tactical frequency while Brutus used his real-life snooping and intelligence skills to search for the tactical frequency that the Hawkeye would be monitoring. Every squadron around the skip had a tac frequency, and most had multiple ones that the jets would use to talk to each other while flying. The Hawkeye squadron usually only had one since they rarely operate in any situation with more than one or maybe two Hawkeyes at a time. There just wasn't a need for more. That was a good thing for Brutus because it made it easier to find. Rattler sat in the front of Bronco and looked at his Breitling. He knew they were running out of time, and he needed to make this happen now or his friend would be at risk.

"Any luck?" Rattler asked over the ICS.

"Just found it, sir. We are up on their frequency. I just hope they are listening," Brutus replied.

In the back of the Hawkeye, Brucie sat in the middle between two other NFOs. She was the overall mission commander, and this was likely one of her last flights in-country before returning home to Point Mugu. She was already having a successful skipper tour and likely would continue further in the Navy. Who knew? Maybe one day she would make the rank of captain and be a Commander of the Air Group (CAG). In a lot of ways, Rattler was surprised she made it so far. Not because she lacked tactical knowledge or ability, but because of the type of leader she was. She genuinely cared for all her people, and while on paper that was what the Navy said it was looking for in their skippers, Rattler knew that wasn't a quality that always got you promoted. In many cases, it was the men and women who put their people first that often got passed over for promotion. Brucie had worked hard and was right where she belonged. Rattler just hoped that he could convince her tonight that Maestro was in danger.

"Cyclops, are you up on tac?" Rattler radioed over the frequency. He waited and heard nothing. Over the dark skies in mountainous terrain, trying to avoid being detected by both sides of the war that had been raging for decades, both in theater and on the news, Rattler could only hope that someone in the Hawkeye heard his radio call and would respond.

"Cyclops, are you up on tac?" Rattler radioed again.

"Go for Cyclops," Rattler heard.

"Cyclops, is Cyclops actual onboard?" Rattler replied. He needed to talk to Brucie directly, and he hoped that she would respond. He knew that his call was a bit unorthodox, but so was everything else that he was doing these days, so why would his radio calls be any different?

"This is Cyclops actual," Brucie replied.

Rattler recognized her voice immediately. He had spent plenty of time with her in the past at the Fallon Officer's Club or while both squadrons were home from deployments in Point Mugu. She was a soft-spoken woman who knew how to be stern, and from what he remembered, she also had a zest for life that few embraced. She knew how to work hard and play hard, and while others normally couldn't balance that, she did it flawlessly.

"Brucie, is that you?" Rattler asked.

"Yes," Brucie replied.

"Great. We don't have much time, and I really can't explain. I need you to trust me here," Rattler radioed back. "I need you to confirm that Hellcat one-two is Maestro."

"Um, who is this?" Brucie radioed, clearly confused about what was going on.

"That isn't important right now! I need you to confirm that Hellcat one-two is Maestro, and if so, I need you to redirect him with different tasking. This is a time-critical order and needs to happen now!" Rattler replied. As soon as he did, he knew he screwed up. Being stern with someone like Brucie would likely send her down a path of doing things completely by the book. He didn't know what else to do because he couldn't reveal his identity, so he was hoping she would just follow the order.

"I am going to need you to authenticate yourself, and we need to switch to a secure frequency," Brucie replied.

"Unable," Rattler radioed back. "Listen, I know this is strange, but listen to your gut here. I know you are someone who wants to do the right thing and also someone who believes in good and evil. Hellcat one-two is going to be targeted tonight, and you need to direct him to one kill box south of his location. If you don't do this, he is a sitting duck and won't know what hit him."

"Okay, even if I listen to you, which frankly I'm not sure that I can, what about Hellcat one-one?" Brucie asked.

Rattler knew that question was coming, and he was prepared for it. "Okay, listen, and I will make this quick. We are running out of time. We spoke once back in Point Mugu after I returned from deployment and found out I was getting a divorce. I was pretty down, and I ran into you downtown. You told me something that I still remember today. You said that in life we cannot control everything around us and that sometimes things happen that are bigger than us and out of our control. When things like that present themselves, we just have to do the best we can with the information we have at the moment and make a decision. Then we live with that decision and move forward. This is one of those moments, and I need you to make the right decision. Maestro's life depends on it," Rattler finished.

"Who is this?" Brucie radioed back, in shock because she remembered who she had that conversation with, but she also knew that person had been shot down months prior and was dead. Chills ran down her spine as she started to sweat in the back of the Hawkeye. She had always been able to keep her composure, but she felt dangerously close to losing it right now. She didn't know what to do as she tried to listen harder to the radio. There was no reply. She turned down all the other frequencies, hoping she didn't lose radio contact. She was just about to give up when she looked at her scope and found Hellcat 11 and 12 operating in their designed kill box.

"You need to listen to your gut on this one, Brucie. I know you'll do the right thing, and you can call me 'Ghost' because I'm back from the dead," Rattler radioed back and then switched frequencies. The mission was about to start, and he could only hope at this point that he said enough to convince her to redirect Maestro out of danger.

"Sir, it's starting. Hellcat one-one just got back from the tanker. He is in the kill box and filled with fuel. His jet is the least maneuverable it will ever be. The mission is a go," Brutus called over the ICS.

CHAPTER FIFTY

Sitting alone in the Hornet, Maestro was messing around with checklists and listening to the chatter on the radio from the SEALs on the ground. Often during times like this, he wondered how he got here. A lifetime ago, he never would have imagined he would be flying a fighter jet above the sky in support of special warfare commandos on the ground. His jet had five hundred rounds of 20mm in the gun and two five-hundred-pound bombs—one laser guided and one GPS guided—under the wings. While not as much as some of the Air Force big wing bombers, he could unleash a hell of a lot of power in a short time, if needed.

Despite all that, it was hard not to think of home. He missed his family and just wanted this flight to be over. After landing, the ship would turn and head home. His was the last mission of this deployment, and with all that had happened, he was ready for it to be over. It was a six-month deployment, but it felt twice as long. Losing a roommate had that effect. He scanned his instruments; everything was in order. Checking his displays, he could see that Toad was on his way back from the tanker, and soon it would be his time to go. Only a few more hours and he would be back on the ship, getting some food and then some sleep.

Brucie broke the radio silence. "Hellcat one-two, this is Cyclops on your tac."

"Go, Cyclops," Maestro radioed back.

"Maestro, this is Brucie. I know this sounds weird, but I need you to flow south after hitting the tanker. I repeat do NOT return to your kill box. I can't explain further, but I've received a radio call from someone, and for some reason, you need to be out of that area ASAP," Brucie replied.

"Huh? Who called? What's going on?" Maestro radioed back.

"Standby," Brucie replied. She had no intention of radioing back. She had already done all she could without completely going against the regulations. She was listening to her gut, but at the same time, she couldn't believe the radio call she had gotten. If it had been any other topic, she would have thought it was a joke, but there was something about this that seemed different. She looked to her left and right and noticed that the other crew members didn't seem fazed at all, and they likely weren't even listening to the radio transmissions. She adjusted her scope to find the Hellcat flight and watched. Hellcat 11 was entering the kill box, and Hellcat 12 was heading slowly south toward the tanker track. She said a silent prayer that it would all work out, and she went back to scanning her radar briefly before noticing a small pop-up radar contact just north of Hellcat 11 down low in the mountain range. While watching the Hellcat flight, she tried to keep radar contact on the unknown track, but it was gone.

Maestro was listening for Cyclops when Toad radioed back.

"Hellcat one-one back on station. You are cleared off to get gas," Toad radioed.

"Copy," was all Maestro said as he turned his Hornet south and started toward the tanker.

His mind raced as he tried to make sense of the unorthodox communication. Part of him wanted to tell Toad, and another wanted to try to get Cyclops back on the radio, but a voice inside of him told him not to. He would be out of the kill box for fifteen minutes getting gas before he decided what to do. It would be very strange for him not to come back to his flight lead. He needed time to think, so he pulled his throttles back slightly to slow down. *No need to get to the tanker too fast*, he thought.

CHAPTER FIFTY-ONE

Rattler eased the stick back to hold altitude in his orbit. The mission was coming together, and he hoped he had done enough to help his friend. He also hoped that he didn't overstep his boundaries as the new guy in the organization. But what was done was done, and there was nothing he could do about it. Toad was in the kill box, and the guys on the ground were working to ensure everything was set for the barrage of missiles they were going to send his way. One small part of Rattler felt bad. He never thought he'd go against his own squadron mate and fellow naval officer, and now he was doing it for a second time. It felt different with his Hawkeye skipper because his skipper tried to kill him. Rattler had to remind himself that Toad did as well. If all had gone according to their plan, Rattler would have flown into the water after the night catapult shot where he lost all of his electronics in the Hornet. When that didn't work, they effectively shot him out of the sky in hostile territory, and if it wasn't for Mundus Tutor stepping in to rescue him, he would likely have been killed on the ground. Rattler had read all the intelligence and after actions reports, and frankly, he would not have believed any of it if he hadn't seen what these people could do. Their connections ran deep, and they could seemingly reach out and control anyone's fate anywhere. He would not let that happen again. Toad was at least one head of the snake of the organization, and while Rattler wasn't sure how involved Toad was—if he was as involved at the same level as his Hawkeye skipper or had a larger role—it didn't matter. It ended tonight.

As Rattler listened to Brutus give updates from the back of the Bronco, he thought about how relieved he was that Clipper was responsible for the pickup. He knew Toad was a great pilot and would likely evade some of the missiles, but they would eventually get him, and Rattler was happy that he didn't have to be part of the pickup crew. If he had to face Toad, it would likely get personal, and he wasn't sure how he would act. Once that switch was flipped, he wasn't sure he would be able to turn it back. He had already changed throughout all of this, and he was a man with a lot less to lose at this point. His safety was not something he was concerned about, and while he would fly the Bronco to the best of his ability, he had no real reason to worry about his own mortality.

Rattler's anger rose as he tried to focus on the tasks of flying the plane and being ready to go at a moment's notice. All systems seemed to be working fine on the Bronco tonight, and it flew very easily. He was on his NVGs and staying low around the mountain ranges. He stayed in his prebriefed area to be close enough to back up the pickup but far enough away to not be in any danger of getting in the way of the SAMs that would be unleashed.

One thing that he found a little challenging was staying low. He was not expecting an AWACS as well as the Hawkeye to be flying around, and with both radars, he knew if he wasn't careful, he would pop up on one, and one of the airborne early warning aircraft would likely send a fighter to check him out. That would blow the whole mission, so he spent a considerable amount of his attention just making sure he was flying low, but not too low, to minimize the risk of hitting the terrain. Nobody would win in that case.

"Sir, it's time," Brutus said from the back.

"Copy," Rattler replied over the ICS as he said a little prayer for his friend, silently hoping he was far enough away to be clear of the missiles and nothing went wrong. *It will all be over in a few seconds,* he thought.

CHAPTER FIFTY-TWO

"Hellcat one-one defending missile in the air," Toad screamed over the radio as he grabbed the stick and throttle of the Hornet and tried to get a visual on the missile targeting him. Instinctively, he hit the jettison button and got rid of his two five-hundred-pound bombs and two external fuel tanks, making his Hornet much more maneuverable. Once the call came out, radios went crazy with people trying to figure out what was going on. None of that mattered to Toad as he hit the chaff/flare button, trying to get the one missile he saw to track on a decoy. If he could just get away from that one, he would be able to fly low, egress the area, and link up with Maestro to regain his section integrity. Having someone else help him would be a huge asset.

A hard pull to the left and more flares were the last things it took to defeat the first missile as it tracked aft and exploded, temporarily blinding Toad due to the overexposure of his NVGs. As he regained his sight, he saw that his jet was still screaming at him that more missiles were in the air. A scan left and then back right over his shoulder yielded three more SAMs lifting simultaneously, all tracking him. He heard no communication because he was too busy to do anything but fall back on his training from years of being a Navy fighter pilot. He knew energy was life, and he did everything he could to keep speed on his jet to be more maneuverable. If he got too slow, he would be a sitting duck for any more missiles that were sent up. He was pulling massive amounts of G's while making his flight path

201

unpredictable and trying to keep his engines out of the afterburner detent. He had no idea if the missiles were heat or radar guided, but none of it really mattered. He was flying like a man who was trying to save his life.

Toad looked over his left and right shoulders, back and forth, trying to keep his sight on the missiles, because he knew if he lost them, he was toast. The NVGs helped a lot in this case, and he noticed one missile seemed to stop tracking him and fall off to the south. A second missile detonated prematurely far behind him, which meant he only had one left to defeat. He focused on it and checked his aircraft systems. He was getting low on chaff and flares, as he had been pumping them out as quickly as he could to provide decoys. His aircraft confirmed what his eyes saw: there was only one left. If that was it, he could use more of his energy to defeat the final missile and get the hell out of the kill box.

The entire time, his radios were screaming at him with everyone from Cyclops, the AWACS, as well as the SEALs on the ground talking to him. None of it actually registered, and to Toad, it was insanely quiet as he danced with the missile in a life-or-death tango that he was winning. As the final missile approached, he timed it perfectly to break hard and into it while pumping out the last of his decoys. A smile crept across his face as he saw it explode off to the left of his aircraft.

For the first time since the first warning, Toad exhaled and relaxed for a second. He took a quick inventory of his jet and fuel. He was low on gas again and out of chaff and flares. It looked as if he had over-G'ed the aircraft slightly, but it was flying okay. All seemed well, and he was about to turn south out of the area when he was met with an audible warning from the aircraft.

"Engine left. Engine left," the Hornet complained.

As Toad scanned his jet, he could see the left motor oil quantity was reading near zero, which would likely result in having to shut it down. With his mind still on overload, he knew he needed to get his energy back. He was dangerously slow from his last-ditch effort to defeat the final missile, so he took the left throttle to idle and the right throttle to max and brought the plane around to the south. Just as he was going to key the radio to make the mayday call, Toad looked in his mirror to see if there was any visible damage from the left motor. In the darkness through his NVGs, his world stopped as he was met with the reflection of a small aircraft. It wasn't Maestro nor any plane he was used to seeing. As he brought the left throttle back up to maximize the plane's performance and rolled the aircraft to the left to dive to the deck, his reality became clear. Everything was happening in slow motion. One final thought came to mind as he tried to will more out of the jet and pumped the chaff/flare button in hopes that there was something left. "SHIT!"

CHAPTER FIFTY-THREE

Rattler listened on the radio while the action went down, but he really didn't need to. With the help of the NVGs, he was close enough to watch each missile launch and follow through the sky as Toad defeated them, one by one. He listened on the radio as the guys on the ground, acting as SEALs, tried to help Toad out, but he doubted Toad processed those radio calls. Rattler figured it was over when they launched three SAMs almost simultaneously, but then one went "stupid" and veered off course, and another detonated prematurely. It was at that moment that Rattler knew he would be the organization's last-ditch effort if Hellcat 11 defeated the final missile.

"Brutus, get Clipper up on the radio!" Rattler called over the ICS.

"Standby, sir. He has been redirected to go after the SAM that went stupid," Brutus replied. "Not sure if he will be able to do the pickup, so we need to be ready for that. Start looking for a landing spot while I coordinate."

Rattler watched Toad in Hellcat 11 pump out more chaff and flares and thought he must be getting low. He wouldn't be able to outrun a Hornet, so he started to get himself into position. It was hard to predict which way Toad was going to turn because it seemed like he was just doing anything he could to save his jet. In the back of the Bronco, Brutus was busy trying to coordinate a flex game plan. He didn't notice that Rattler was trying to will the last missile to impact Hellcat 11, to end this once and for all, but his prayers wouldn't be answered. Toad aggressively banked his jet, and the missile detonated aft, leaving Toad safe, even if only momentarily. Without thinking, Rattler cycled through the weapons pages on his OV-10 and pulled up the AIM-9X system. Immediately, missile cueing was brought up in his helmet display as he maneuvered his Bronco into position. He would only have one shot at this.

As he came around and pulled the nose up, he saw Toad right in front of him. Toad's jet hung in the air, and Rattler realized he was completely out of energy. He had used all his airspeed to defeat the missiles, and he needed to get his nose down to be able to fight, but for a moment, he just hung there. Something had distracted Toad, and it gave Rattler a huge opportunity.

During flight training and while getting ready for deployment in the Hornet, Rattler spent a lot of time doing simulated air-to-air fighting, and he had a pretty good working knowledge of the energy states of aircraft and when an aircraft was offensive versus defensive. The Hornet was an amazing machine and could almost defy the laws of aerodynamics at times. Unfortunately, that was not the case for Toad right now, as his nose was up and his power was too far back. His only option was to lower the nose and jam the throttle forward in hopes of gaining some speed back, but one more thing was working out for Rattler. He didn't think Toad had spotted him yet.

As the nose of the Bronco came up, the cueing locked onto Hellcat 11. Time slowed for Rattler as memories of his aircraft emergencies flashed into his mind. He thought of all the times these evil bastards had tried to kill him. He thought about his parents and how he would likely never get to see them again and how they must have felt when the Navy sent a chaplain to their house to tell them their son was dead. He thought about all the others affected by the power-hungry treasonous assholes who thought they were untouchable. Finally, he thought of how Sandy must have felt lying on the side of the street, bleeding to death alone, and how he would never see her beautiful smile again or feel her touch. In a lot of ways, he died with her that day, and he had been reborn as a man on a mission of revenge. A man who had cold blood running through his veins and anger in his heart—the type of anger that may never be fully resolved. He gripped the stick tighter as he pulled the nose around a few more degrees, applying more G-forces to the Bronco and causing Brutus to finally realize what was happening.

"Whoa. What are you doing?" Brutus asked over the ICS.

"Fox two," Rattler replied out of habit from his Navy training as the AIM-9X came off the wing of the Bronco on a mission to finish what the SAMs could not. Rattler closed his eyes to shield them from the flash of the exhaust from the missile and was met by the vision of Sandy smiling at him in a way he would never forget.

CHAPTER FIFTY-FOUR

"Okay, I have a marker beacon from the seat," Brutus called from the back of the Bronco. "Right side about three o'clock low."

"Tally, keep eyes on him while I find a place to land," Rattler replied.

The AIM-9X had met its mark and flew right up the tailpipe of Hellcat 11 as Toad tried to do anything he could to evade. Nothing mattered at that point, and as the jet broke apart, Toad knew it. While Rattler maneuvered the Bronco out of the path of the stricken Hornet, he saw Toad make the final decision to eject. Memories of going through the same thing himself just months before rushed through his brain, and Rattler watched a man who used to be a squadron mate eject into the night sky. The first part of the mission was successful, but now he had to figure out how to get Toad and quickly. He had no doubt that the Navy would be sending assets in to recover their downed pilot, and Rattler needed to get Brutus on the ground quickly to secure the package—or all of this was for nothing.

"Does that look like some sort of road?" Rattler called over the ICS.

"It looks flat if nothing else," Brutus replied.

"Okay, hang on. This is going to get a little rough," Rattler called.

"Now it is going to get rough, sir?" Brutus called back.

207

Rattler banked the Bronco to the right and did his best to line up with what seemed like a road of sorts. This was the type of flying that made him the most uncomfortable. Throughout his career, Rattler had done a ton of crazy shit, but it all seemed very controlled compared to what he was doing now.

"Sir, here is the plan," Brutus directed. "Get me as close as you can, and I will jump out and secure the package. I'll bring him back and get him in the cargo hold, and then you'll get us the hell out of here. Once the Navy sends in their package, this place is going to get busy quickly."

"Copy. I can shut down and help you," Rattler replied.

"I think you should stay with the plane," Brutus answered.

"Bullshit. I'm not sending you out there alone. He will be armed and on the run," Rattler called.

"With all due respect, sir, that guy looked like a tiny weasel in his picture. I'm not too worried about him. But if you get the plane close enough to him, I could use the backup," Brutus exclaimed.

Rattler didn't reply as he adjusted his NVGs to get the best vision of the landing area he picked. The only problem with the NVGs was they lacked depth perception, and he could really use that now landing in the mountainous terrain on an unprepared strip of dirt, but it was all he had. Rattler was in go mode, and his hands and feet worked as an extension of the Bronco. He loved the plane and knew it would be able to handle a rough landing, but he needed it intact so they could take off and get back to the compound. Brutus was right about the Navy and likely Air Force assets, which were likely already homing in on Toad's position. They didn't have much time to mess around before this place would really get out of hand. They were operating alone here as well and would likely be considered unfriendly forces to anyone they encountered, so they needed to avoid that at all costs.

Rattler slowed the plane as Brutus's eyes scanned the area to find where Toad hit the ground. Brutus would keep his eyes on Toad while talking to Rattler to help him land as close as possible. The closer they were, the quicker the pickup could be. As Rattler slowed to extend the gear, Brutus gave him one last update.

"If you were any closer, you'd land on him. Land the plane, stop, and do a one hundred and eighty degree turn. He will be on the right side just along the tree line," Brutus said.

"Got it. Standby and hold on. Here we go," Rattler replied as he wrestled with the Bronco, which was catching crosswinds from the mountains around them. When the wheels hit the ground, Rattler was relieved to feel that the ground seemed solid enough. Rattler leaned hard on the brakes, spun the OV-10 around, and brought it to a stop. Almost before the aircraft was fully stopped, Rattler heard the canopy open, and with a flash, Brutus was out and tracking Toad.

Chapter Fifty-Five

Rattler shut down the plane as he saw Brutus slowly move to the right, his rifle at the ready position. Creeping low, Rattler pulled off his helmet and left it in the plane. Now wearing a black ski mask and drawing his Sig from the holster, he followed Brutus slowly. His brain tried to focus his eyes on the outside world. It was brighter than he expected, but it was also dead quiet. Rattler could only hear his breathing and heartbeat as he tried to control both.

Now, just slightly left and behind Brutus, Rattler paused, scanning for Toad. He knew they were operating in no-man's-land, as this portion of the mission was an extreme backup. If Rattler were to really think about it, everything that could have gone wrong had gone wrong. They'd had to leave one Little Bird back at the compound; it took far more missiles than anticipated; and now Rattler's final intervention to get Toad on the ground was not going as planned either. Clipper was retasked to get to the site of the SAM that went stupid to destroy any evidence, which left Rattler and Brutus to bring Toad back. Prior to exiting the Bronco, Brutus said he saw movement, which meant it was likely that Toad had survived the ejection. Now they had to find him and find him quickly. Rattler was doing everything he could to mirror Brutus and not get in the way. His area of expertise ended when he exited the Bronco, and while he was fairly comfortable with the Sig he was holding, he also knew that Brutus had spent far more time on the ground than

Rattler ever had, and because of that, he deferred to the expert. He was in backup mode and decided to stay slightly behind and to the left of his friend to cover his flank. He knew Toad would be armed, and if he was conscious, he would be extremely confused and likely think that anyone coming to get him was the enemy. Rattler had no desire to do anything that could get himself killed or hurt at this point.

Both men scanned the distance, looking for any sign of Toad. Rattler's senses were becoming more honed in the darkness, and every sound got his attention. Time slowed, and he noticed the calmness that his friend exuded. Brutus was in his element and knew his role. He needed to find Toad at all costs and get him aboard the Bronco and into the cargo hold. Brutus was far bigger than Toad, and there was no doubt in Rattler's mind that Toad would be convinced to get on the plane by any means necessary. He wondered if this scenario was similar to how he was picked up after getting shot down. He had no real recollection of the events that happened after he pulled the ejection handle of his Hornet, and for all he knew, they picked him up in a very similar fashion. Although Rattler did believe he was unconscious during the events.

At any rate, he could see Brutus's movements as they advanced closer to an area on the side of the road that would make a good hiding spot. Although Rattler didn't realize it, Brutus was on the scent of their mark and had already noticed that the road was disturbed and shrubs were broken, leading him to believe Toad was close. Brutus took each deliberate step with his rifle at a ready, scanning left to right slowly with his finger off the trigger, but ready nonetheless. Rattler tried to control his breathing, but it seemed futile. Nothing seemed to be working, so he just accepted that he wasn't in his element and focused on providing cover for Brutus. With his Sig at a ready, he mimicked his team member, and while seconds seemed like days, he knew they needed to find Toad quickly because the Air Force and Navy were likely jumping into action and redirecting all assets to descend on the area to recover their downed pilot.

Rattler froze at the sound of movement to the right. Time stood still as Brutus scanned the area. He had a bead on the area where he believed the mark was, and like a trained Labrador retriever, he was not going to let anything get in his way. Rattler noticed Brutus had moved his finger to the trigger of his rifle, but before he could think about that, the silence was broken.

"We are a QRF sent to pick you up, sir," Brutus yelled into the darkness. "If you can hear me, I need you to come out so we can get you out of here."

More silence as Rattler wondered if this was going to work. He was trying to put himself in Toad's shoes and determine how he would react. Rattler realized that was impossible because he was not the treasonous shithead that Toad was, so Toad very well might be more on guard than Rattler would have been. Rattler figured that confronted with the same situation, he would have put his weapon down and come out of the hiding spot. That is what they were trained to do in a situation like this. There was no need to provoke the rescue team into thinking you were an enemy combatant. In fact, pilots who had done that in the past found out quickly how the rescue team would react and none of them wanted that.

Finally, after what seemed like a lifetime of Brutus staying completely still, facing the darkness in silence, Rattler saw movement. Toad slowly stood and moved forward with his gun at the ready. Rattler could see he was fairly beat-up after the ejection. He was wearing a Navy-issued flight suit but had no patches, name tag, or rank on it. His helmet was gone, as was his survival vest and G suit. He'd likely stashed those somewhere when he heard Brutus and was now making his way slowly toward them, with his gun trained on Brutus.

"Sir, I need you to put down your gun and authenticate yourself," Brutus yelled.

Silence from Toad as he processed the scene. Two commandos dressed in all black were holding guns at him in the mountainous terrain that seemingly only minutes ago he was flying above. Rattler almost felt bad for him because he knew no matter how good Toad was, he was definitely dazed and confused and was trying desperately to process what was happening. He wanted this to be a quick reaction force sent to save him. He wanted to be safely back in the hands of the military and headed back to the ship. He likely wanted to go home, but none of that was going to happen.

The more Rattler thought about it, the angrier he got about all the hurt and pain Toad had caused and how he had done it under the ruse of being a loyal squadron mate and even a friend. All the time they'd spent together in the ready room or briefing spaces preparing for missions was all complete bullshit. It was just part of the plan for Toad to ultimately end Rattler's life—a vendetta created by the circumstances around his former mentor from the Naval Academy. Rattler felt the switch flip inside of him now clear as day as he saw the man responsible for trying to kill him as well as Sandy's death. The rage welled up higher than it ever had, likely because he was now face-to-face with the enemy. Rattler knew how this was going to end. His focus was clear, and his aim was true.

"Sir, please put down your gun. We need to get you out of here." Brutus's gun was trained on Toad's, and the two men stood off like in a western dual. However, Rattler knew that one movement from Toad and Brutus would put him down for good. "LCDR Troy Kirby, sir—we are here to take you home."

With that, Toad snapped out of his frozen stance and lowered his weapon. Brutus's bluff worked, and Toad followed his directions to place the weapon on the ground and kick it away. In a way, Rattler couldn't believe Toad was listening, but at the same time, Rattler would have likely done the same thing confronted with similar circumstances.

"Sir, I need you to walk slowly toward me. We need to move deliberately but quickly to get out of here," Brutus said, and Toad complied. To Brutus, the plan was coming together, albeit slowly. He knew that once the mark was close, he would be able to subdue him quickly and get him into the Bronco. Rattler would get them back to the compound, and this would all be over. A sense of satisfaction swept over Brutus. He knew that although they were the backup, they did their jobs, and the mission would be a success. Another enemy of goodwill and freedom would be put away forever.

Brutus lowered his rifle and let it hang from the sling as Toad moved almost within reach. That's when he noticed Toad's gaze had moved to his left. Brutus saw Rattler had removed his ski mask. The two advisories' eyes were locked. Toad looked as if he were seeing a ghost, while Rattler's expression was pure rage.

Chapter Fifty-Six

On the side of a road in a mountainous region in a land where war had been commonplace for decades, two men stood facing each other—men who were connected by a greater bond than they could ever know. Good versus evil was represented that night in a land forgotten by so many. On one side stood a man who tried to do his best, serve his country, and make his family proud. A man who had seen loss and pain but moved forward in hopes of making a difference. On the other side stood a man who had lost his way. At some point, he went from the side of good to the side of self-service. A man who lost faith in the system, who cared only about how he could make things better for himself, and who stopped caring about the greater good. Although unknown to both, their paths were set to cross many years prior, and now, at this moment, with a bright moon in the sky, their destinies would be determined.

Brutus looked at Rattler, who still had his Sig trained on Toad's center of mass. His finger was on the trigger, and he could easily end this at a moment's notice. Brutus also noticed something else. Rattler was different. He was changed by the pain of war, and the pain of loss. Looking at Rattler's eyes, Brutus saw a different man, a man who had already lost everything and therefore had no reason to hold back.

Toad and Rattler stared at each other, not saying a word. Toad's brain tried to process what he was seeing. Up until a moment ago, he thought Rattler was dead. He had to be dead; there was a body.

215

Now, as his brain slowly processed the truth, Toad realized this was not a quick reaction force. This was not his ticket back to the ship, to his home, and back to his normal plan. Standing in front of him, Rattler represented the end of the road. There was no way out unless he went through both Rattler and Brutus, and that wasn't going to happen with both men armed and his gun somewhere in the dirt behind him. Desperation set in as his brain tried to figure a way out. Before he could, Rattler made a move—a move that confused both Brutus and Toad.

"Here," Rattler said to Brutus, lowering his Sig and handing it over to his friend.

"Sir?" Brutus took the gun and repositioned his hands onto his rifle to be ready for whatever happened next.

"Didn't expect me?" Rattler asked Toad.

Toad finally spoke. "You're dead!"

"Then it's time for you to fight a ghost!" Rattler replied.

With that, Toad lunged at him, catching Rattler off guard. Both men tumbled to the dirt in a heap, trying to gain the advantage. Rattler was bigger, but Toad was a man with no way out and nothing left to lose. He needed to somehow take out two men at once, but right now, Rattler was the enemy. Since they first met, Toad had been on a mission to eliminate Rattler, and he had failed many times. The higher powers that controlled him were very unhappy and threatened to cut him off. Toad had gotten used to the finer things in life, and he couldn't afford any of that on a Navy salary. Additionally, Rattler was responsible for killing Toad's mentor. Ever since the day Maddox died, he was on a path to pay back Rattler for what he did. Long before they even met, Toad hated Rattler and knew this day would come. Months prior, when Rattler was shot down and a body was found, Toad was upset that he would never get his chance to kill Rattler himself. Now he had his chance, albeit a small one.

Both men wrestled on the ground, trading punches and kicks. At one point, Toad got behind Rattler, and Brutus tried to find a place to shoot, if necessary, but Rattler was like a shield protecting Toad. That is until Rattler made a defining move and head-butted Toad. Instantly, Rattler was free and on the attack again, and this time, he wasn't going to give up the offensive. He'd been taught in air-to-air dogfighting that if you have the offensive position, do everything in your power to never give it up. That's where Rattler was at now.

Two quick punches and Toad staggered, and Rattler closed the gap, wrapping his left arm around Toad's neck from behind. Sensing he was losing, Toad fell back, causing Rattler to lose his balance and fall to the ground, but he never let go.

Instead, lying on his back with Toad on his stomach, Rattler tightened his arm around Toad's neck. Toad sensed the outcome and made a final push to try to get away, but Rattler used his size to his advantage. All of Rattler's days in the gym, coupled with his extreme anger, ensured Toad had no chance of getting away.

Rattler swung his legs on top of Toad's to lock them in place, and then he squeezed tighter. Unable to breathe, Toad's body convulsed and struggled, but to no avail. He knew he would pass out if he didn't do anything, so he reached his right hand up toward Rattler's head and eyes and tried to get ahold of anything at all that would cause Rattler to let go, but Rattler arched his back to keep his head out of reach.

For a moment, Toad felt like he was losing consciousness, but then he got a breath of air. He couldn't believe it, but something caused Rattler to loosen his arm and gave Toad a chance. Momentarily stunned, he tried to figure out what to do with his window of opportunity. He thought Rattler was weak and should have never gotten to fly fighters, because when push came to shove, he would cave. Toad knew this in his heart all along. He knew Rattler didn't have the warrior spirit to fight in his core. He knew Rattler was a loser. Before he could think too much more, Rattler tightened his arm again and drew his face close to Toad's ear.

Rattler had slid his right hand behind his back and found the Speedgoat knife exactly where he put it. No matter what he had been through that night, it was exactly where he needed it, the ultimate wingman, as Rattler reached behind himself and found the 550 paracord handle and drew the knife. With Toad's right arm still extended upward, Rattler had a clear shot at his axillary artery. From school, he knew there was a vulnerable spot in Toad's right armpit. With all of his rage, he tightened his grip around the handle and drove home the carbon blade three times into Toad's side.

"This is for Sandy; I want you to feel her pain," Rattler whispered.

Toad's pain was instant, and Rattler knew he had hit the mark based on how Toad's body reacted. He had opened up an artery that was now actively pumping the evil blood out of his enemy's body. With every drop came salvation and closure. Rattler held tight until he was sure that Toad was dead. Then he wiped the blood off the blade onto his flight suit, released his grip, and fell back. His job was done.

CHAPTER FIFTY-SEVEN

The men moved slowly in the darkness. Once again, just like on the mountain road months prior, Brutus took the lead and Rattler followed slightly behind and to his left. While the area should have been heavily guarded, most of the security guards were occupied at the north end of the estate. Sensors were going crazy, showing motion from the perimeter, working as a distraction to give Rattler and Brutus a red carpet to the front door.

Brutus moved quickly, disposing of any targets with his suppressed rifle while Rattler provided cover. Even in the darkness, Rattler was impressed by the size of the estate. Clearly, the owner was a very wealthy man—a man Rattler knew was not looking for any more money but instead thrived on power. That power was what made the blood run through his veins. He could buy anything he wanted, but from the looks of things, he already had it all. Power was the only thing that would quench his thirst.

Brutus was a man on a mission. Being picked to lead this mission was a huge step in his life. This was the ultimate high-value asset, and he knew that Mr. Gray and Clipper would not have trusted him if he wasn't ready. Regardless, he planned and overplanned for every contingency. The main unit of distraction moved in from the north hours ago, providing a minor nuisance to encourage the guards to let down their watch. After several hours of checking on the motion that was seemingly coming from animals, they'd relax. Then the main contingent would start their move. They would be met with very little resistance at first, but once the shooting started, it would draw the guards on the south side. This would leave Rattler and Brutus with a clear shot into the mansion.

Unlike their last major mission together, this one was going off as planned. Once the north contingent broke through the perimeter of the mansion, their main job was to gather intelligence to bring back to the organization. After that, their objective and target were the same as Brutus and Rattler's, although the way things were going, Rattler knew they would get there first. As he approached the steps up to the front door, Brutus took down two guards with four shots so neatly placed that Rattler wondered if Brutus had been a surgeon in a previous life.

Once inside, both men heard muffled sounds coming from the north side of the house—if you wanted to call it that. They were keeping up with how the plan was progressing through the secure earpieces they each wore. Both men tried to focus as they made their way through the house by memory to find the objective. They had prepared and studied and knew the layout like the back of their hands, assuming the intelligence was right. So far it was. One final turn and the men faced a large, heavy wooden door they had dubbed "home plate" in the mission brief. Brutus confirmed this over the secure communications as the men pressed forward, Brutus in the lead and Rattler behind and left as they moved as one.

Brutus approached the door and tested it to see if it was unlocked, which it was. When you are a man of such power, you feel untouchable. Given the extreme ego of the owner of the house, it did not surprise Rattler that he left the office door unlocked. It may have been an oversight, but Rattler thought that was unlikely.

With a nod, Brutus went through the door and to the right while Rattler followed and turned to the left. A quick scan confirmed that the room was empty except for one person. The mark sat at his desk, flanked by two computer screens. The arrival of the two intruders didn't seem to faze the old man as he sat in his lush chair in a very relaxed manner. A moment after Brutus and Rattler entered, the old man reached across his desk to retrieve a sip of what Rattler could only imagine was an expensive and rare beverage.

"So, here you are," Ronald Daggett said. "Now what?"

Rattler had moved closer and dropped his rifle to the sling. While Brutus had closed the gap to the desk, Rattler drew his Sig, which was now silenced with the silencer Brutus gave him months prior on the other side of the globe, from his side holster.

Neither Brutus nor Rattler spoke.

"Well, if you aren't going to talk," Daggett said, his gaze moving to Rattler, "then I will. We all know how this ends, son. It is apparent to me that you have chosen your side. That became very clear months ago when we found the body of LCDR Kirby left on the side of the road near where you were shot down, if I'm not mistaken. Seeing you here face-to-face tonight tells me that our intelligence might need to be readjusted slightly, moving forward. With that being said, you have clearly only heard their side of things, but this is when I have a chance to tell you our side."

The words had barely left Ronald's lips when the contents of his brain exited the back of his head and took their final place on the wall behind the desk. Two 9mm rounds of silenced ammunition found their mark so accurately that one could wonder if the second one even hit anything since the first did all the destruction.

"This isn't that type of story," Rattler said out loud after pulling the trigger.

EPILOGUE

The all-gray BMW 5 series backed into the residential driveway in a neighborhood that Rattler knew very well. It was just after dawn, and they were a block away from the house where Rattler grew up. It was a middle-class neighborhood in the New Jersey suburbs where, frankly, the BMW wouldn't look too out of place, if not for the dark, black-tinted windows. Otherwise, its presence just indicated someone trying to live outside of their means and keep up with the Joneses.

Rattler sat in the passenger seat as Mr. Gray put the car into park. From this distance, Rattler couldn't see his childhood home, but he had long since stopped asking questions about where they were going and why they were here. Now he just sat in the car, taking in the nostalgic sights from a lifetime long ago, when innocence ran through his veins. It had since been replaced with rage and then vengeance, and now Rattler sat just taking it all in. Since the final mission, Rattler had laid low, kept training, and got checked out to fly the Little Bird helicopters, something he never thought he would do. While he enjoyed being a pilot, flying aircraft that had zero glide ratio wasn't as appealing. Over time, he realized that the Little Birds were used often on missions and tended to get assigned the more exciting tasks, while the OV-10 tended to work in a support role. Not counting his now legendary air-to-air kill of an F/A-18C Hornet, most of his missions tended to be a little less exciting. Plus, he loved to challenge himself, so when he was approached by Clipper, he took the opportunity. When he wasn't training or on a mission, his free time was spent working out and studying. There was really no time for anything else, and while other people within the organization found love, Rattler was not interested in getting attached to anyone else. He knew the threats of the job and figured it was safer to distance himself. When he needed to find a connection, he pulled up the feed from his parents' house and just watched. He enjoyed the warmer months because his mom and dad tended to spend more time outside. Whether he was watching his dad mow the lawn or his mom play with their two dogs, it was the closest thing to a connection he had, and he cherished every minute of it that he could get.

Now, sitting in a BMW on the same street where he was born, Rattler wondered if this was the end of the line for him. He knew he couldn't stay in the organization if his parents knew he was alive, and he had heard of some people going back to their previous lives. As he sat on the leather seat, he could feel the uncertainty in the air.

"Look, just get this over with. Why are we here?" Rattler finally asked, breaking the silence.

Mr. Gray handed over a high-tech set of binoculars they often used in the field. Far superior to anything Rattler had used before, the fidelity of these allowed him to lean forward in his seat and see the front of his parents' house clearly. As the sun started to rise, he noticed that the normally empty driveway was occupied. He knew his parents owned one vehicle, which they left in the garage, but there was no mistaking his car. A dark blue 1967 Shelby GT500 with white stripes sat proudly preached, waiting to be discovered. Rattler lowered the binoculars from his eyes and looked at Mr. Gray, who returned his gaze with a nod toward the car.

Rattler knew the car well but had never seen it in that condition. Even from a distance, he could see the detail of the restoration was second to none. The last time he'd seen it was when he carefully backed it into a storage unit before leaving on deployment. Studying every inch of the beauty, which was a gift from his father many, many years before, he found himself getting emotional seeing the condition it was in. He noticed movement and saw his father walk slowly out the front door with a cup of coffee in his hand. He scanned up and down the street and moved toward the car, slowly examining it. Rattler knew right away that someone as smart as his father would not only know the type of car right away but also know that it was the exact car he gifted his long-lost son. His father circled the car numerous times, taking in every inch of it while stopping to look up and down the street to see if anyone was around. Confident that no one was around in the early morning, his father put his hand on the hood. From this distance, his father appeared emotional. Mr. Gray started the BMW and inched forward. Just before they turned away from his childhood home, Rattler saw his father look up to the sky like he'd seen multiple times from the drone footage.

By the time they turned the corner and were back to normal speed, Rattler had finished processing what he just saw. For the first time in what seemed like forever, he spoke.

"How . . . why did you do that?" Rattler asked.

"It's what your father needed. I understand that what has happened to you is beyond hard, but you are an asset. One day, you may make it back to this street and back to your prior life, but right now, your parents needed that. When I started the organization, it wasn't to take people away from their loved ones; it was to protect them. I would love more than anything to turn around and drop you off at home. I know your parents need and want that, and I know you feel the same, but you are an asset to this organization, and for the time being, you are in the right place. One day, I will bring you back here for good, but first, we have work to do."

THE END